From a very young age Charlie had a vivid imagination, she was always creating stories. There was always a story on the go, no matter what.

During her time in school, she found a love for English Language which spurred her on to take it at A-Level and then at Degree level. With a BA (hons) English Language and Linguistics she now teaches English to those who need it.

Teaching and writing are a nice balance. But she also pursues her other passion which is horses. In the end, Charlie would like to write full time, giving her the time to write more and the freedom to ride her horses.

I dedicate this to:

Mum, Dad, Paula and Barbara.

Charlie Tallentire

BASKERVILLE

AUSTIN MACAULEY PUBLISHERS™

LONDON • CAMBRIDGE • NEW YORK • SHARJAH

A CIP catalogue record for this title is available from the British Library.

ISBN 9781398495661 (Paperback)
ISBN 9781398495678 (ePub e-book)

www.austinmacauley.com

First Published 2023
Austin Macauley Publishers Ltd®
1 Canada Square
Canary Wharf
London
E14 5AA

A massive thank you to Austin Macauley Publishers for seeing the potential in my writing and of course, Usman Maravia – without his support and proof-reading Baskerville would never have been finished.

Preface

Baskerville was a small unimportant part of the new America. It was where the unimportant people were sent, and it was where unimportant things happened. The courts were always empty, and the laws were always abided, as everyone was scared to do anything wrong.

Thing was, in this world everything was wrong and there was no freedom. There were strict rules about how to live life, and if these rules were broken, then the punishment was death. End of the road. It did not matter how serious or how awful the crime was, the punishment would be the same. Being hanged, while the whole town came to watch and cheer.

In the whole of Baskerville history, there have been 5 hangings. This was very little. It was something that, as a town, Baskerville was proud of.

Baskerville had concluded that the reason for their success was because of how their rules controlled the population. Everyone had a life plan that they were given by the government, and one that they must follow. They were given a house, a car, and a partner. They were given everything so that they could live a life serving Baskerville. There were no decisions that need to be made, as they had already been made for them. Baskerville believed that this was the key to their success, as everyone was happy with the life that had been given to them.

Baskerville worked in a way that meant the more you did for the town, the better you did as a person. So, if you worked in a high-paying job where you put your life on the line for the country, then you would get a better house and a nicer car and live in the nicer part of town. However, if you were sorted into the manual labour side of the town, then you would get a smaller house and a not-so-nice car and live on the rougher side of the town. In some ways, this system was fair, and if you worked hard there was always a way to better yourself and get a promotion. But if you came from a labour family, it was very hard to work up to the better side of town.

No one would ever bother the people within Baskerville because of what they did to gain this independence. America granted them their independence after the great war, and it would stay like that till the end of time. There was no question of it. Baskerville was free to do whatever it wanted, and nothing was going to change that.

Many years ago, there had been a great war, that included the whole world, it had gone on for so long that it got to the point, that people forgot what they were fighting for, and countries forgot whose side they were on. People were simply fighting because they could, and they had been told to. This war had lasted whole lifetimes and it was something that had become the new way of life. That was until a small corner of America decided that they were going to end the war. They released an announcement to the whole world, using the most futuristic screen through space, that projected all around the world explaining what would happen if the war carried on. Baskerville owned something that other countries didn't.

Baskerville had nuclear.

They never directly threatened the world, but it was made clear what they could do, should they decide to do it. With the threat of a nuclear bomb that could annihilate the whole world, hanging over their heads, the world came to peace, and they settled their differences and stopped the war. Baskerville was very quiet throughout the settling and asked only to be left alone. They never wanted to be bothered. They would be considered their own country with their laws. They would have nothing to do with the USA and they would not abide by their laws. This was, of course, agreed to and the world carried on. Baskerville was never mentioned again.

If you look on world maps or even look at an in-detail map of the USA, you will never see Baskerville. They have been removed from all maps. There is no record of them existing and you cannot travel there. From an outsider's perspective, it does not exist. And to those who live there, the outside world does not exist. Baskerville is its own entity and nothing or no one will ever be able to change that.

Chapter 1

Boris Cleave was one of the higher-paid residents of the Baskerville community. He had been given the job of the monitor when he left school, which meant that he had the job of keeping an eye on the community and making sure that everyone was sticking to the rules. Because of his job, Boris was not well-liked in the community. Obviously, they knew that it was not his choice, but they still resented him slightly for what he did. But he managed to make a life for himself in this weird world.

Boris was one of the few residents who had managed to work himself up to the higher residential part of Baskerville. He had started on the poorer side of town, and over his lifetime had worked himself up the ranks, from Chimney sweep to Head Monitor and this was something that he was very proud of and something that he told anyone who would listen, he was not ashamed, no matter how people spoke to him.

When he was first paired with his partner, they did not get on, but as time went by, they started to fall for each other and after a couple of years they fell in love and got married. This was nearly unheard of in this town, because of the way that the couples were created, but this couple had love, real love and it was a rarity. So, when their daughter Amy came along, they were genuinely ecstatic at the news.

Amy Cleave was a bubbly little girl and all through school she was consistently at the top of her class. It seemed that there was nothing that she could not do. She loved school and put everything she had into it. This meant that when she was offered a position in monitor school, she was happy to follow in her father's footsteps, after seeing how successful and happy he had become within that lifestyle. It was an exciting time for her to go forward and onto something that she wanted to do. She wanted to do it to make her father proud, but there was also a part of her that felt that she deserved it after all the work she had put in at school. She wanted to do just as well within monitor college as well.

She had worked hard in school, she had handed in every paper and taken notes on every class. She was eager to get into to monitor college so that she would be able to live up to her dad's expectations. She wanted to make him proud, but she also had this feeling deep down inside of her that she was never enough for her parents. She needed to do this so that her father would be proud of her. She needed to become part of the monitor college so that she could follow in her father's footsteps, it was the only way that she would be able to stay in the part of town that she was accustomed to. If she had not worked so hard within the school, there was a risk that she would get given a low-class job straight from school and would be given a house within the low-class area of the town.

This was something that Amy knew her father would not stand for. He had worked hard to get his family up into the upper side of town and he would not be able to sit there while it all disappeared. Amy knew that she had to keep up her father's reputation and the only way to do that would be to join monitor college. This was why she was so pleased when she got the call from the college to say that she had been accepted, as long as she gained the grades needed.

Boris, naturally, was very pleased when Amy was accepted into the college and was full of praise when the letter arrived. This was something that Amy took great pride in. It was very rare that she would get praise from her father simply because of the kind of man he was. His job came before everything, even his family, and this was something that Amy had had to adapt to during her childhood. She knew that her dad would never love her the same way that he loved his job and that was just the way that her father was. There was no changing him. Amy almost admired him and the way he had put his whole life at the mercy of his job.

Without his job, Boris was not the same man. He needed to be a monitor to carry on working for the country and helping the other monitors rid the country of criminals. Amy could never understand how her father was so busy, as it never seemed as though there were any criminals in Baskerville, but Amy supposed that was because her father did his job so well, that the criminals did not dare cross him. This was another reason Amy wanted to be a monitor. She wanted to be able to change the world that she was born into. She wanted to make a positive difference to the world and ensure that the residents of Baskerville were able to live the life that they chose. Rather than being confined by the rules.

Amy had never been very good at following the rules as she believed that they were restricting and did not allow people to follow their dreams. She wanted to live in a world where you could be anything and that was just not Baskerville. It was too restricting for Amy, but getting the higher paid job on the right side of town was a good start for her if she wanted to change the world.

Chapter 2

Amy awoke with a start, she had a minute and then remembered that today was the day that she would start monitor college to follow in her father's footsteps. She was nervous and excited as she packed her stuff into the car. Not only would this be her first time away from her parents it would be the first time that she would be able to fully understand the world that she lived in. Monitor college was only on the other side of town, but the students there were required to live in while they were studying. This allowed them to gain the full experience of what being a monitor was like, and meant that the students could gain a fuller education that allowed them to meet people that they would be sharing their journey with.

Amy was glad of this, as it would allow her a little freedom from her parents. She had been living with her parents her whole life, so, naturally, they had been involved in every part of her life. Amy thought this would be a good next step for her, as once she had finished monitoring college, she would be given her house and her partner for life and then expected to live off her own means. This was a good middle ground, to get her used to living in a world without her parents and their support.

Baskerville ran by different rules to the rest of the world, and everyone let them. This was because of how they ended The Great War and put the world to peace. They were allowed to run using their own rules and no one would say anything to them. It was because of these rules that Amy was off to the special college. Because of her high grades within high school, she had been selected to become a monitor within the community. A monitor was someone who would keep an eye on the community from within and inform the authorities if someone was caught breaking the rules.

This was the most acclaimed job within Baskerville, but it did not come without its challenges. Because of the way that the monitors had to give up people within the community, they were not always liked, and sometimes feared.

People understood that they had not chosen this life and that the government just gave them that job, but they were still not liked, as the community had to blame someone for the way the world was, and they chose to blame the monitors.

When Amy finally arrived at the college, she was shocked to discover how small the college was. She could not understand how a place that was so important to the community, would be so small. She dragged her bags out of the car and ran up the stairs to unpack. She was eager to meet people like her that did not know what they were in for or what the future held for them. It would also be a chance to meet the people that she might be partnered up with for life. Within Baskerville, people did not choose who they were to marry, they were simply put with someone, and that was the end of it. There was no divorce or separation in Baskerville, you stayed with who you had been assigned.

This was the strange thing about Baskerville even with all the strange rules it did seem that the government was quite talented at pairing people with others who would most complement their life. This was a skill that had been perfected over time. Not allowing residents to choose their own life partner, meant that the government had complete control over who was talking to who. This also meant that they could genetically modify the town to make it more sustainable. It was highly controlled, and no one made their own decisions. The people of Baskerville never questioned or challenged this way of living, because to question the government was classed as treason, which was a crime, and all crimes were punishable by death.

Even though the monitor college was based just on the edge of Baskerville, it was mandatory for the students to board at the college. This was to ensure that the students were not influenced by the outside world while they were within the college and to stop them from getting distracted from their studies. Their rations were taken away from their families and they were fed solely by the government. Living in was something that Amy was nervous about. She would be on the full government diet. She had always eaten what her mother had managed to cook out of the rations that the house had been allocated at the shop, but this diet was different.

It was designed to keep the monitors fit enough to do their job and have enough nutrients in their diets to have the energy and alertness, but there was nothing more. This was to ensure that they did not put on any weight and would only consume the exact number of calories that they needed. Amy was worried that she would struggle with this, as she was known for eating a lot. Her mother

15

had always managed to keep her going with the rations that they had been given. She was worried that she would not be able to do the job on the food that the government deemed fit for her. But this was something that she was going to have to adapt to, as she would be here for some time eating this diet.

The first morning within the halls was a strange one. Amy got dressed and headed down to the breakfast hall. She had never been a big breakfast fan but now that she was officially on the books, she did not have a choice, she would have to become a breakfast person. All the food that came out of the chute was specially formulated for each individual. By scanning the bracelet that was given to Amy at birth, she was able to gain her meal which had been carefully calculated by her height and weight and how demanding her job was, which worked out exactly how many calories was needed to last to the next meal. No more, no less. The residents had always been fed this way, but it was more apparent within the college, because every meal was monitored rather than just the usual daily allowance.

The breakfast that was served was a simple oat mash that was apparently the best thing that you could eat in the morning. Amy recognised it as what her dad ate for breakfast every morning. She presumed this was where he had discovered it. As she looked around her new surroundings, she began to realise that she had been put into a job that only accepted the elite of the community. She had been grouped with the best of the best within the town. This job was going to be both interesting and scary.

Looking into the dining room there was a group of people on each of the tables, so choosing which table to sit on was a big decision. Amy managed to choose a table where the people looked normal and approachable. They greeted her in the usual way, but one girl caught Amy's eye. She was so unbelievably pretty that she took Amy's breath away. She had no idea what to say to her to make her sound cool or make her seem like someone that this stranger would want to be friends with.

Amy had never been that good at social situations she always overthought every exchange she had with other people, and she had always been extremely nervous around other girls. Most of her friends were boys, because of this and it was how she had managed to get through school, because of her talent within the school football team, the boys had always been willing to take her under their wings. She got on with the boys as there was no fuss with boys. They were not the same as girls.

Girls were picky and had a way of judging you before you knew them. It was this that Amy could not stand. The first time she saw other girls, she struggled to explain herself and get her point across. They would laugh at her because of her awkwardness, and she could never get on. But she was going to have to try within this college, she had decided and made a deal with herself that she was not going to be awkward this year. This was a new start for her, and she was not going to mess it up. She was going to put herself out there and try to gain some girlfriends, as she definitely lacked them.

"Hi, my name is Amy, is it okay if I sit here?"

Amy was so nervous about talking to this girl and she couldn't understand why. It was like she had some sort of power over her that Amy did not understand but she sat down next to her, and they talked whilst eating dinner. Amy learned that she was called Emma and she had also been selected to be a monitor, which was why she was at monitor school. She was the same age as Amy and had just left the school on the other side of town and came straight to monitor college. Just like her. The more she talked the more Amy realised that they had in common.

They both wanted to be at monitor college. Amy wanted to be there because of her father and Emma wanted to improve herself and allow herself to go up in the world. Although they were both from very different parts of Baskerville, they were very alike. They were both driven and eager to finish Monitor College and gain a job within the government allowing them to earn the money and the house of their dreams. They both discussed this over breakfast and how they were planning to do well within the college. It seemed they both had the same ideas.

After breakfast, they walked to the first lesson together.

Throughout monitor college, Emma and Amy were inseparable. They were never apart. It quickly became clear that they were very close and were going to be friends forever. They got on so well and never argued, it was only when graduation came around, that problems arose. They would have to separate when they were both allocated partners and a house as well as an area to monitor within their new duties. Neither one of them could imagine having to separate, and they didn't want to. Amy knew that they would still be able to stay friends, as they would be in the same neighbourhood due to having the same job, but there was something else.

Something deep down inside Amy knew that she didn't want Emma to be given a partner, she didn't want Emma to be given a house and a car and go about her business with this partner. Amy wasn't sure if she wanted to be the partner or whether she just didn't want to share Emma. But there was an uneasy feeling inside her that made her question everything within her life. Did she want to have Emma in the way that she was supposed to want a man? Or was this just not wanting her life to change?

These feelings began to eat away at Amy. She did not know what these feelings were, but she knew that it was not normal. She and Emma were not in a normal relationship. They were closer. Closer than friends should be. They had something else going on. She was just not sure what that something else was, or whether it was something she would ever be able to pursue.

Graduation came too quickly. The day was a lovely one. The sky was blue and all the students who had finished monitor school were queueing up to receive their outfits. Amy was nervous. This was the day when her whole life would change. She had now finished monitor school. She knew that she had passed as she had already gained her results. She had passed with the highest of honours. She could not believe it, but she knew she had worked hard, so why should she not gain the results that she deserved? It was just the idea of leaving Emma. She did not know how she would be able to cope without having her by her side every day.

They had been together for three years non-stop; how did the college expect that to just end? Just because they had finished college. The whole idea was preposterous. The idea of just simply disappearing from each other's lives now that they had finished college. This thought made Amy feel a little bit sick. She walked past the lady and gave her name before getting her outfit. She would just get through the graduation and then bring it up with Emma, and they would discuss everything together.

As the ceremony started, Amy could not the question out of her mind so when she saw Emma, she didn't know what to do with herself. Because of this, she just stood very quietly next to Emma and didn't say anything.

"Are you okay? You haven't said a word to me all day?"

Emma had clearly noticed that there was something wrong with Amy and in her own straight-talking way, had just come out and asked the one thing that Amy didn't know how to answer. She could feel a tightness within her, but that was all. Just this nagging tightness that she did not know how to control. She would have to speak to Emma about it, but there was simply no time. They would have to sort this out after the ceremony and see what could be done.

"You feel the same as me, don't you? And you don't know what to do. I don't know either but it's something we will deal with once we have graduated, I promise."

Emma could sense that Amy was wrong. She knew that there was something going on. There was something going on and she knew what it was about because she felt the same. She had the same tightness and weird feeling in the pit of her stomach. Maybe it was just because of how close they were, or maybe there was more to it than she thought, but she knew there was something that they needed to talk about, it was just when would they find the right time?

Both girls sat in silence during the rest of the graduation ceremony. Apart from when each other's name was called, when they made so much noise to make it known how of each other they were. There was something about the graduation ceremony that made everything feel so final for everyone that attended. But it was even more final for Amy and Emma, they were at risk of being separated and were about to be paired with their long-life partner whom they would have to spend the rest of their lives. This was something that Amy could not imagine now, she did not know if she was gay or if it was just Emma, but she knew that she didn't want to be with anyone else.

She could not imagine being stuck with someone who was not Emma, day in and day out. Even if she was partnered with Emma for work, which was still so unlikely, it would not be enough. Amy wanted to be with Emma in a way that was more than friends. She wanted to be with her in a partner sense, in the same way, that she should be wanting a man. This was something that Amy knew was wrong. She knew that Baskerville would never allow such relations. She knew that it was banned within the country and how her family would react should they find out.

She could not understand what was happening to her, but Amy knew that she could not deal with the idea of Emma being partnered with someone who wasn't her. She didn't know how she would cope without Emma and the idea of sharing her was heart-breaking. Amy hadn't given too much thought about herself, but as the date drew closer for her to be assigned her new partner, Amy began to realise that this was not the life that she had wanted. She wanted to be with Emma and there was nothing she could do.

Amy knew that she was going to have to sit down with herself and think about what she wanted out of life, before she spoke to Emma. She needed to know where she stood in her own head before she started to make decisions about her life. She knew that she needed to sit and think about everything before she spoke to Emma. She needed to know how she felt before the issue arose of what was going on within her head. At this moment in time, she did not know what these feelings were, or how she was going to control them. She just knew there was something not right between them, and that the idea of being separated was killing her inside.

After graduation, there was a two-week wait for the residents to gain their house and car and be set up with their new partner. This was a time for the students to prepare for their new lives and to enjoy their last days with their parents. Amy and Emma had been camped out at Amy's house during these two weeks, as her house was bigger, and the girls wanted to spend this time together. Emma did not mind spending the time away from her family, as her family did not get on the way that Amy's did, and being with Amy for those two weeks, uninterrupted, was the only way that Emma could think about spending this free time.

Amy's parents did not mind either, as they knew how close the girls were. Boris always said there was nothing more important than children having friends within this world, so when Amy asked if Emma could stay for the two weeks, he obviously obliged. So, during these two weeks, the two girls were inseparable. They didn't leave each other's side and spent every waking moment together. They did a lot of discussing, but never seemed to get anywhere as to how they felt about each other.

Amy knew how she felt about Emma she just didn't know how to get the feelings across to her. She didn't want to have the conversation and then be rejected. Having to admit to herself how she felt to then have her feelings thrown back in her face without warning. She knew that she wanted Emma in a way that she was supposed to want men and she knew that this was not allowed, she knew that admitting her feelings would not only put her in danger, but it would put Emma in danger and that was not something that she wanted to do. She knew how she felt now, and she knew she had to tell Emma, but she was not going to put Emma in danger for the sake of saying it. Amy was at war with herself. Did she tell Emma, or did she just try and let it go and be happy that they were friends?

The morning before they had to sign on for their new life was the morning that Amy had decided that she would approach Emma about her feelings and discover if she felt the same.

"Emma, can I speak to you about something?"

Amy had never been so nervous. This was the biggest moment of her life so far; it was bigger than any of her exams and a lot bigger than being assigned. It was the only thing that she had thought about all through the break and it was the only way that she wanted to live her life. She wanted to live her life with Emma.

Emma looked worried as if she knew what Amy was going to say, she had also been feeling something, but she had known straight away what the feelings were. She knew how she felt and what she wanted out of the relationship, she just didn't live in the right town to be admitting these kinds of feelings. She knew that they would both be hanged if they were found out. She knew that this was not something that she wanted to happen.

The disappointment that the town would feel, never mind her parents, was overwhelming. This was something that had to be handled carefully, it was something that was going to have to be dealt with. They had come too far to not say something to each other, but it was the aftermath that Emma was scared of, what would happen if it did go too far and they got caught. She did not want to put Amy in danger of any sort and it was this that scared her.

"Amy, I know what you're going to say, and I love you too, but we have to be careful with how we go forward with this, as we can't do it. It's against the law, we will get hanged if we get caught. We have to be careful."

Amy was shocked, she couldn't understand how Emma could know or how she had managed to understand her completely without Amy ever mentioning anything before. She couldn't understand how someone could be so in tune to her to understand what she was trying to say before she even knew herself how she truly felt.

"You know? And you feel the same? So, it's not just me, I'm not mental we do have something going on here. I haven't imagined it; we do have something special."

"Yes, we do have something, I just think we need to be careful. We still need to carry on with life, we still need to imagine that everything is normal, and nothing is out of the ordinary. We have to carry on otherwise we are both going to end up on that stage and we can't do that to each other."

Both girls were stuck, they had finally admitted how they felt but they were powerless to do anything about it, they had to just carry on with their lives knowing that they both felt the same but that nothing could be done for them. It was an evil and slow version of torture.

Amy thought telling Emma how she felt would make it all easier but learning that she felt the same just made it even more difficult. She didn't know what to do, she had no way out of this and could not imagine life without her. Amy didn't want to live a fake life with her husband and pretend that she was enjoying her life when it was so clear that she wasn't.

She wanted to come out, fully, and tell the world who she was and what she wanted out of the world. But that was not possible, if she admitted that then she would be hanged. No questions asked, being a homosexual was against the law, and that was it. There were no special privileges, they would just have to try and get on with their lives and try to pretend it had never happened.

Their last night together was an emotional one, they both knew they would be assigned tomorrow and would have to carry on as if their feelings didn't exist. They would have to carry on and just imagine that their love was not real. They would be assigned partners and a brand-new life away from each other and then live out their days apart. They only had this night left together and both girls were going to have to think of a way to live with that for the rest of their lives. This was it. This was all the time they had left together. 12 hours. 12 measly hours.

So, they made their final night count, they laid together talking for hours, putting the world to rights.

Just before Emma was about to go to sleep, Amy leaned in. She knew this was her last chance to show her just how much she loved her. She wanted Emma to know that even though the world was against them she did still love her, no matter what the world said.

Amy leaned into Emma and Emma sat up, she knew what was about to happen and was eager to receive it.

"Are you sure you want to do this? It could ruin our whole future?"

Amy sat a while and thought about it, she didn't have a choice. She could either have this night with the woman she loved and remember it forever or sit and think what if for the rest of her life.

"Yes, I'm sure, I don't want to be with anyone else."

Amy leaned into Emma once more and their lips touched for the first time, there was a spark between them that could not be ignored, as soon as their lips touched it was clear that this was the true love that people spend their lifetimes dreaming about. This was the first kiss that everyone wishes that they have. The one that they write songs about. This was the relationship that both girls had been dreaming about for weeks. But this was the relationship that was illegal in their state. There was no getting away with it, and there was no way that the relationship could carry on, they would have tonight and then had to forget about each other.

Emma broke the kiss first and began to work her way down Amy's body, it was like she had done this many times before and knew exactly what to do. Amy felt like a fish out of water and completely out of her depth, but she was just glad to be so close to the woman she loved no matter how short the encounter would be. Emma had a way of making Amy feel safe even within all this craziness. As Amy began to relax, she began to feel things she had never felt before, a sudden warmth spread around her body, and she began to wish Emma was even closer, closer than she had ever been before.

As Emma worked down Amy's body Amy began to moan, she knew she had to be quiet with her parents only next door but the pleasure of it all was taking over her body. Having the woman, she loved touching her made her feel all kinds of things, but she had never felt freer.

"Are you sure you want to do this?"

Emma was unsure that Amy was willing, she had gone limp, Emma was eager to carry on but did not want to hurt Amy's feelings. There was a feeling of finality with this like there was no going back. Ever.

"There is nothing I want more."

Amy could not imagine not going through with it now, she was ready for Emma to do what she wanted with her, she was waiting for her. The two girls had been waiting for this for many weeks and were eager to get to know each other. They both wanted to live their lives like this, but it was not possible they would have to be satisfied with this one night that they had together before they would have to carry on with their lives. There was a certain pressure on this night and both girls knew it, if they did not do this now, they would never be able to. This was their one chance to feel each other and be together. Both girls had become subdued to the pleasure that this encounter was bringing, and they could not think about anything else.

Emma proceeded further down, reading Amy's pleasure, she knew she was doing right by her reactions and how her actions were being received. She could see the pleasure in Amy's face, and she knew that she was close. This was all that she had wanted for so long. She had wanted to be with her for so long that it had all just exploded when it had eventually happened. From this, they knew that they were meant to be together, they knew that this was love, but they were powerless to do anything against the state.

As Emma found Amy's point Amy began to convulse in such a way that made Emma understand that she was nearly on the edge. Amy moaned and grabbed Emma's arm, she was close to the edge, and she knew it. She had never been here before, and she was fairly sure that she would never be here again, not with someone else. As Emma carried on working, she could feel the explosion building up inside her.

As the explosion erupted inside Amy it was a warm rush through her whole body. She wanted to return to Emma but couldn't move. Amy felt as though her whole body had been abused but in the most amazing way. Emma reappeared from under the covers and kissed her in such a way that finished her off. Amy cuddled up next to Emma and sighed. She had no idea how she was going to live without this girl.

Amy didn't want to break the moment. The magical moment that they had just shared but she was aware that there were some things that needed to be spoken about before tomorrow rolled around. She knew that as soon as her name was called her life would be over forever and she would never again be able to see Emma in this capacity ever again.

She did not know how she was going to get through it, but the idea of Emma going through the same thing would help her through. They were going to face it together and make sure that they were still able to be friends at the end of it all. They could never be more than friends, but maybe, somehow, they would be able to stay friends within the craziness of this world.

"What do we do tomorrow?"

Amy was anxious to hear if Emma had a plan for the rest of their lives and how they were going to carry on knowing what they knew now.

"We carry on as if nothing ever happened, it's going to be hard, but we don't really have a choice, we just have to carry on with everyone else. And imagine that this didn't happen."

Emma knew that it was going to be difficult, she knew that ignoring this was going to be easier said than done. They would have to carry on as if nothing had happened and would be assigned partners and their lives in the morning.

When morning arrived, neither girl wanted to get out of the room. To leave the room would mean that they would have to put themselves forward for this new life and have to try and ignore what had happened the night before. When they walked away from that room, they were walking away from their relationship. They were walking away from everything they had shared and walking away from any potential relationship that they were able to rekindle if they somehow managed to get away from this crazy town.

Chapter 3

As they walked down the path, from Amy's front door, it was clear that it was two girls walking towards the end of a complicated relationship. They were preparing to change their lives completely and to say goodbye to their feelings for each other. Amy did not know how she was going to carry on without Emma and being with her every day, but she knew that she had to, for her father's sake. She did not want her dad to know that she had wandered from Baskerville life and that she wasn't the dream citizen that she should be.

She had worked her whole life to make her father proud and although she loved Emma more than she ever knew was possible there was still the side of her that wanted to make her father proud. She wanted more than anything for her dad to be proud of her and Amy knew this was the moment when she might finally say 'well done' to her. She was not about to mess that up, it could be one of the biggest moments within her life.

As Amy arrived at the village hall she got into her queue and prepared to meet the man that she would have to spend the rest of her life with. How was she going to be able to carry on knowing that someone else would-be touching Emma? She would have to live with the fact that someone would be doing all the things with her that Amy wanted to do. Life was not fair in Baskerville, and it was now when Amy felt it more than ever.

As other people's names were called Amy's imagination was pulling her into all kinds of visions of Emma with strangers. All of them created more and more anger inside Amy. By the time it came to her turn, Amy was furious. She did not want anyone coming anywhere near Emma, let alone being the man in her life and taking control of her. She could not allow that. She did not want to see that happening. She especially did not want to sit and watch it happen in front of her eyes.

"Amy, if you would come up to the table, please."

The sudden realisation that she was about to be given her life partner brought her back into the real world. Amy did not know if she was ready for this. But it was too late. She was going to have to walk up and gain her life. She could do this, she was sure.

The lady had called her name and she walked up to the table; she gave Emma a look that could only say I love you. As she walked to the table, she knew that her life was about to change, she knew that she would struggle to carry on, but she would have to, she did not have a choice.

"Ok Amy you have been paired with Max, you will live at number 44 Upper Drive and your car will be parked outside. Max is already stationed there and waiting for you, enjoy your life."

"Thank you, I can't wait."

Amy had never lied to anyone before but this was only the start of her deceit, she knew that she was going down a dark road, and for her, she couldn't see the way out.

Walking into the new house, Amy had no idea what to expect. She knew that her new husband Max would be waiting eagerly to meet his new life partner, but Amy could not face the prospect of having to live with someone other than Emma. She looked at her new life partner and had no words for him. She did not know what to say to this poor person who had been paired with her, she was now going to have to live a lie for the rest of her life.

He was not a bad-looking lad and in any other circumstances, Amy was sure that she would have been happy with the man that she had been assigned. But it was never going to be him, not now that Amy had experienced what real love was like. There was a part of Amy that was starting to wish she had never met Emma. If she had never met Emma, then she would be happy right now. She had got through monitor college and had been placed on the good side of town. Her life was good at the moment, it was just a shame that she would not be able to spend this time with the person who she loved and who she wanted to spend the rest of her life with.

Max had already put the kettle on and was preparing to make a cup of tea. He seemed nice, but Max just wasn't Emma and Amy could not get this out of her mind.

"Hi, my name is Max, I've been paired with you. At least we have a house on the better side of town, I was worried that we would be stuck on the rough side with no prospects."

Amy did not know what to say to this. She was incapable of explaining the feeling that she was having. How would she be able to tell her father how she was feeling now she was finally living the life that she had wanted since she first started dreaming about her future. Even she did not understand what was happening, she knew that she did not want this life, she wanted a life with Emma, and this was all she knew.

"Yeah, at least we have a nice house and stuff. I'm just glad I managed to get through monitor college, I thought I had failed that last exam for sure."

Amy tried to relate to this boy that she had been paired with, as she wanted that more than anything. She wanted to be able to understand him and try to have some sort of feelings towards him, but in the end, Amy knew that this was not going to happen. She was not going to be able to fall in love with this man. She was not going to be able to give her heart to this man. It was just not possible; her heart did not belong to her anymore. She had already given it to someone. Someone was already in possession of her heart, and there was no way she would be able to get it back now.

Chapter 4

Months had passed, and Amy had settled in well into her new job and new house. She was struggling with her job, but she was getting through, she had a notoriously difficult job, and she was allowing time for that to come. But there was one thing that was not becoming easier, her love life. Amy had tried with Max she knew that her parents had managed to fall in love even though they had just been assigned to each other, so she knew it could happen, but whenever she tried to imagine having a normal life, she always had Emma by her side, it was never Max. This was becoming more and more difficult, she was stuck in the mindset that she needed this girl, and she could not shake the feeling that she belonged with this girl, not with Max who was trying so hard.

Amy almost felt bad for Max as he was trying so hard to ensure that she was happy. He was always asking her if she was okay, and he would make tea some nights. He even did all the washing up as he knew how much she hated the feeling of the food in the water. He was completely perfect. There could not be a nicer boy within Baskerville, but he was being wasted on a girl who would never feel the same. He was wasting his time, and she was wasting his.

Amy did feel bad, as in an ideal world he would have been perfect for her and together, they could have proved Baskerville wrong and fallen in love. But this was just not the love story that Amy had imagined. She was now going to have to live with the knowledge that she was stuck with this boy forever and there was nothing that she could do that would change that.

Amy had a tough week that week and was struggling with getting to grips with all the protocols that had to be adhered to. When she got home, she discovered that there was no food in the house, as she rummaged through the cupboards looking for something to cook, she decided that she would have to go shopping. This would not be fun as the upper side shop would be shut by now which would mean that she would have to go to the other shop on the other side of town, which was always full of the wives of the workforce.

These were the uneducated women of the town and women that could only cook and clean for the men that did the manual labour in the town. It was chaos. It was also risky for Amy to go to this shop. As someone from the upper side of town, she would be targeted and the poorer people within the community would be able to spot her a mile off. This was a risk she was going to have to take as all her cupboards were empty and she had to eat. She checked that she had her bracelet on and got into the car. Shopping in Baskerville was anything but easy.

Now that she had moved out of Monitor College, Amy had been given a food allowance. This allowance was tracked on a bracelet that all Baskerville residents wear. The idea of the bracelet was that it calculated how many calories you burn off in a day and then how many calories you will need to gain the energy you need and maintain the same weight. It was all down to maths. The bracelet did other things but predominantly it was used to monitor food intake.

Once you were partnered with someone, the information would be transferred to your partner's bracelet meaning that anyone within your household would be able to pick up the allowance for that household without having to have their own personal bracelet. This was the one thing that worked well in Baskerville. Especially when you come to have a big household. But there was just Max and Amy within her house so she would only have to pick up two lots of allowances.

The shops in Baskerville were not like the shops in other parts of the world. They only stocked the essentials and what the government deemed fit for the people to eat. You did not buy food either, you were given your allowance. You would show your bracelet to the person who was manning the desk and they would make you a prepacked bag that had been specially made for you. This allowed the people of Baskerville to only eat what was given to them. It was supposed to stop waste, but it was just another way for Baskerville to control it's residents.

Controlling exactly how many calories a person could eat in a day was another way of the town showing they had full control. You could only shop for people in your household as well. There was no going out to get food for others. To be served at the shop they had to scan your bracelet to ensure that you were who you said you were. This was the only way to get served in the shops within Baskerville. They had to make sure it was you and who was in your household before you were able to get your food.

Amy jumped into the car and drove to the other side of town, she was unaware of how important this trip was going to be, she just couldn't face living this life every day and it becoming normal.

When she got into the car park, Amy could already see that this trip was not going to be the most relaxing shopping trip she had ever been on, not that shopping was ever relaxing, using the bracelet was fine art, and being able to buy the edible food was a first come first serve situation, it was clear she was going to run into some people that were below her within the society. She hated feeling like this and feeling that she was falling into the trap of feeling she was above these people, but the way the world worked just meant that she was.

She locked the car and walked into the store.

When she got into the store, she could not believe her eyes. The woman that she had been avoiding for months was standing there looking at her the same way that Amy was looking back. Both girls were shocked but ecstatic to see each other. Neither one of them could hide their emotions, it was clear that they needed to be with each other. Amy felt all her emotions, that she had bottled up for the past few months, come bubbling back to the surface. She felt like she could cry just stood looking at Emma. She needed this girl back in her life.

"Hi, you look amazing. What sort of house did you get assigned? What is your partner like? Mine is nice and easy to live with. I don't think we will ever get on like we're supposed to but he's kind and easy to talk to which is more than I could wish for."

Emma was excited and could not hide it, she was happy to see Amy and could not find the words to explain herself. All the words just came gushing out, she could not stop herself. She did not even take a breath in between her questions. She was too excited to even give Amy a chance to respond.

Amy was taken aback by all the questions that had just been thrown her way. She knew that she had been ignoring Emma but she thought that it was understandable. They had decided to go their separate ways when they had been assigned their partners. They knew that they would not be able to coexist normally, so they had decided to try to simply get on with life without each other. Amy knew she should have reached out in the end and tried to speak to Emma but she knew that she would not be able to control herself if she did. Amy knew that she should apologise for treating Emma this way, but she had no idea where to even begin.

"Hi, sorry I haven't been in touch, I didn't know what to say and I felt like I needed the time away. I can't cope with this life; I can't cope with living a lie."

Amy didn't know how to explain how she truly felt in front of Emma, she couldn't even explain how she felt to herself. She knew deep down, but there was always a part of her that was never sure which parts of the city were bugged. She did not want to go into a love confession here in the supermarket carpark, where it was very likely, there were cameras, or even worse, microphones.

"Don't worry I completely understand, I have been in the same situation I just can't seem to get past these first awkward instances with him. We just can't get on the way we are meant to."

Emma seemed to fully understand what Amy was saying as she was going through the same thing that she was.

"Do you want to get out of here?"

Amy had no idea what she was suggesting but she knew that she had to be alone with Emma. She knew that if she did not comply with her urges, they would eat her alive. It was animalistic what happened when Amy was close to this woman. She could not control her urges. It was like she had been taken over by another force.

Both girls rushed out of the store and into Amy's car, Amy quickly started up the engine and drove it onto a small corner on the other side of the street where they would not be disturbed. Amy turned off the engine and quickly jumped into the back of her big and expensive car. She had never enjoyed the size of this car until now. Emma quickly followed her into the back and jumped on top of Amy. Both girls were overcome with desire, they were enjoying being touched again and just being together. Emma was kissing Amy in a way that she had not been kissed in so long. Both girls were wrapped into each other like a knot.

Their bodies just fitted together; it was the only thing that felt right for them. It was the only way they could ever imagine being with someone. Amy convulsed as Emma started to undress her, she had no idea how one girl could have such an impact on her. She loved this girl and could not imagine living her life without her. Both girls' feelings immediately rushed back to the surface, it was like they had never been apart. They were meant to be together, there was no denying that. It was like they were destined to be together., no what the odds. Both girls had been sent to each other and it was obvious that after this, they would not be able to be apart again.

The girls were finally together and at that moment, it was like there was no one else in the universe. It was simply Amy and Emma that we're finally together. Both girls were suddenly oblivious of the outside world. They were not thinking about the cameras or the microphones or the punishment that would surely follow if they were ever caught. They were purely caught in the moment with each other and were enjoying every second.

As the girls became more comfortable in the back of the car Amy began to lower herself towards Emma's point, Emma could feel what she was doing and began bucking uncontrollably. She had been waiting for this for months. Amy worked her way down past Emma's breasts and towards her point, she was as eager to get there as Emma was. She could not think of anything better than to give Emma the pleasure that she had been craving.

As Amy worked on Emma's point, Emma began to moan, she was screaming Amy's name as she worked it to her advantage. As Emma came to her close, Amy slowed the rhythm and allowed her to take advantage of the feeling, she wanted to prolong her pleasure for as long as she could. As Emma finished, both girls let out such a large sigh, which brought their situation back into reality. This was all a dream, and the reality crushed them like bugs.

Both girls led in the back of the car, breathing heavily. With skin on the skin, the girls had not been so close for so long.

"I don't think I ever want to be without you Amy, I don't think I can survive in a world that doesn't have you in it, I don't know what I am supposed to do without you in my life."

Emma was crying suddenly. Amy did not know what she wanted her to say. She hated to see Emma cry, but she was unable to stop it.

"We should run away, get out of this stupid town, in America this is okay, it is totally acceptable, and no one will say a thing, we can live happily, and no one will bother us."

She wasn't wrong, Amy knew that this was the case, but she was also aware of the fence that stood between them and America. The 12ft electric fence was guarded 24/7 by soldiers who were not afraid to shoot as soon as it looked slightly like someone was trying to escape. You didn't leave Baskerville and that was the end of that. It was part of the agreement, no one was allowed to leave.

"You know we can't, it's not possible. I think we have to just try and live a normal life and maybe get together in secret."

Amy knew this wasn't an option either. It was risking too much. If anyone saw them, even the slightest indication, they would be hung. There was no investigation when it came to homosexual activity. One accusation and you were dead. This was just the way it was in Baskerville. It was only like this, because when it came to homosexual behaviour, if there were allegations, it was usually true.

"I honestly don't think we can, it is only a matter of time before someone sees us and knows what we are up to, and then we will be put into prison. I don't know what to suggest babe, we have to think of a plan."

Both girls knew that for them to be together they had to get out of Baskerville, but this was an impossible task. If they wanted to be together, then they must think of a plan.

It was at times like these that Amy did not enjoy her life within Baskerville. She could not understand why, in such a modern world, this kind of relationship was not allowed. It was against the law, that stupid law. The law put a stop to everything that could remotely be likened to freedom. There was no choice within Baskerville, it was a luxury that you could not afford within this city. And it was because of this that Amy and Emma had to get out of Baskerville, they had to get out and enjoy their life, they had to be together, and right now that was the only certainty that was available.

Chapter 5

It was 2 days after the girls had bumped into each other at the shop, there was a meeting at the office and Amy had to be there early as her department was leading this week. She had no idea what the meeting was going to be on. Being a monitor within this community did have its drawbacks. Having to be ready for whatever was thrown at you was something that came with the job, but it was something that Amy did find boring. She found it unfair that she had to be ready for anything within this job, but the job did not have to accept anything from her. This was something that she was struggling with. She had to put her whole self into the job for not a lot in return.

She felt a little as though she was giving her whole life to a cause that gave her nothing in return. She was putting her whole life on the line for the cause, but she was unaware of what the cause was. There was no reason for her to be living life the way she was living it. But it was the only way that it was possible for her to live her life.

As she arrived at the office, she set up the room ready for the meeting. Being head of the department meant that she had to lead the meeting. She had to lead a meeting that she did not know the subject of. This was one of the many challenges that appeared within the job of being a monitor. The things that they do not tell you within monitor college. The fact that the monitors usually did not know the subject of the meeting until they were in it. This was a challenging concept as there was no way to prepare. It was done like this for security reasons which Amy could never see the point of as she was going to find out in the meeting anyway, surely it would make more sense for her to know what she was going into?

Amy was proud of what she had achieved within the department, but she was ready for out, she was ready for something to change within this world. Something to change to make her life that bit more like her life, rather than her feeling like she was living someone else's life.

35

"Amy, I have set up the paperwork for the meeting today, we will set off in 10 minutes. I hope you're ready, this week is going to be a very stressful one, just warning you!"

The boss did not often indulge in what the meeting was about, so Amy knew that this was strange. It must be something major for the week to be stressful, it took a lot for the boss to admit that this job was stressful. If the boss said that the week was going to be stressful, then it was going to be something so far beyond stressful that Amy was not sure if she would be able to deal with the problem.

As the meeting began, all the monitors that were on the higher band began to file into the meeting room. This meeting was not the biggest meeting as it was only for the most confidential information so only the people who really needed to know were included within the meeting. This helped with the security of the monitors and meant that the information was kept within their ranks. As everyone sat down around the table the boss began to walk to the front of the room, Amy was standing at the corner meaning that she could move the presentation on for the boss. When everyone had settled and the room quietened down, the boss began his presentation.

"We are here today to discuss the issues that have become clear over the past few days. There have been reports of homosexual activity within the suburbs and this is something that we must stop. By allowing these people to get away with it, we are showing the community that we allow infringements. This is not something we want to tell the world. Amy, I want you to oversee this as you are living close to where the reports have come from. I want you to take charge and find these disgusting people. I want you to bring them to our attention so that we can deal with them. Does that make sense?"

Amy did not know what to do, she had been asked to head an investigation that she was pretty sure was looking for her. She had no idea how to deal with this, or what to say to her boss. How did she get it across to her that she was fine and that she would investigate this without finding the ending? She would never be able to resolve this case unless she handed herself in.

This was not something she could work with. A shudder travelled through Amy's body. This was the end; she could not carry on after this. Her career was over, and her life was in tatters. She could not come clean without putting Emma in danger, and she could not carry on pretending as someone would inevitably find out that it was her.

She would have to think this through. There was no way she would be able to carry on with investigation and pass off as if someone else was the one that was committing all the crimes. She knew that people did not get away with things like this anyway. She was one of the heads of monitors! She had seen the extent of cameras and microphones that were around the town. There was no way that she would be able to carry on her relationship with Emma and not get caught. Not in Baskerville. It was simply impossible.

Amy panicked; thoughts raced through her brain like motorcars around a racetrack. She was going to have to say something otherwise it would look even worse. She gathered her thoughts and decided she was going to have to power through this just for now while she thought about what she could do. She would have to agree. She did not have any other choice.

What would they think if she refused? She may as well admit that she was guilty if she refused. She would have to accept the job and look happy about it. This was her big break within the monitors after all. This was her first solo case that she had been given full control of. She would have to be happy about it and deal with the consequences after. She would have to come up with a plan, but what plan would be able to help her now?

"Yes boss, that's absolutely fine. I will start the investigation within the suburbs and see if I can discover anything unusual. I will keep you informed if anything comes alight."

She had managed to get across to the boss that she had no idea what the investigation had heard. She had to get the reports and see who had been reporting. She knew that she could not go any further than that as if she asked the people who had made the reports, they would know that they were talking to the girl who the reports were about. This was something she would have to sit and think about as it was not something that she would be able to finish without her community turning against her. This was something that meant she was going to have to get out of this community, she had to find a way to get out of this world, or at least change this world. She had to do something.

"Well, ladies and gentlemen that is all I wanted to bring to your attention today, I wanted you to be aware that there were some serious infringements of the laws and wanted you to be aware that these things were happening. I want us to work together to end these things that are happening within the community. I want this to end now, and I want these people to pay for their sins. I do not want them to be able to get away with what they are doing I want them to suffer the worst death that is possible as it is not acceptable for them to be living that kind of life under our rule. This is something we must deal with now! I want reports next week."

Even the seriousness of the boss' voice made Amy anxious. She knew that the monitors would be taking this case very serious as one of the worst offences within Baskerville was homosexual activity. She would have to come up with a plan and fast. The boss would be onto her very quickly. She would have to come up with reasoning for every decision that she made and be able to back this up with evidence. This was not going to be easy, considering she was the evidence that the monitors would need to quickly close this case.

Amy left the office unsure as to what to do from here. She did not know whether to be happy that it had been given to her as this meant it was under her control, or whether she should be hoping that it hadn't been given to her at all and was given to another investigator who would be able to find her. Maybe being arrested was the best thing that could happen to her. Maybe it was the only way that she could live her truth. She had to go and find Emma and discuss this with her. Emma would need a warning anyway to understand that they were now being monitored. This was something she had to know.

Chapter 6

Amy had to let Emma know, she wasn't supposed to inform anyone of what happened at work, but this was something that would affect them both should it get any further. This was something Amy was going to have to deal with and try and shut them down. It was something she was going to have to try and get the monitors to understand. Amy was going to have to try and figure out a way to get out of this world as they could not stay in Baskerville anymore. Amy was aware of the craziness of what she was forming within her head but she was unable to stop it. She had to be able to find a way for the two of them to escape Baskerville. It was their only hope at being together happily. It was the only way that they could have a happy and normal life.

As much as they were told in school that America was the devil's home and that they were not allowed there for their own safety. Amy knew that she would be allowed to be with the woman she loved if she was in America, and there would be no problem. There would be no issues with them living out their lives peacefully and most importantly together. The more she thought about it, the more her brain was telling her that it was possible. She could do it, even though deep down she knew she couldn't. She knew it was not something that could actually happen.

Amy was trying to convince herself that it was a good thing that she had been put in charge of this case. It was something that she was now in control of and that meant that she would gain all the intelligence about the case. It was just the fact that the boss liked quick results on major cases like this, and that was something that she would not be able to provide, unless she handed herself in.

This was something that she was not willing to do. To hand herself in would mean that she would have to hand Emma in too. Amy could not think of anything worse. She did not want this to end with them both stood on that stage. She had to think of a way out of this situation. They were already in too deep; it was not simply a case of stopping and hoping that it would go away. Now that the monitors were aware of something going on, they would not stop until someone was hanging from the beam. That was just the way that they worked.

They did not let any crime go unpunished, no matter what. The culprit was always found. Amy knew she was going to have to do something. She was going to have to find a way for Emma and herself to get out of Baskerville, alive, preferably, but that was not something that Amy had the pleasure of choosing right now. She just had to get out.

When Amy got home, Max had made tea for her and was sat waiting at the table before he started eating.

"Hi, how was work? Hope it was better than my day?"

Amy was unsure what to say to Max. It was not his fault that he had been paired with someone as different as her and it was not his fault that his house was the monitors most wanted. Amy did not know what to say to him. How did she tell him what was happening without telling him what was happening?

"Yeah, work wasn't too bad, just the usual day. I think I am going to go out tonight and try and calm down after a stressful day. I just feel like I need a walk."

"Yeah, no worries, give me a bell if you need me."

An awful feeling surrounded Amy about what she was doing to Max she was supposed to be open and honest with her husband. She was supposed to involve him in all decisions, but she could not include him in this. It was far too sensitive. If he found out the real reason for her lying to him, he would never forgive her. This was something Amy was going to have to sort out herself. She could not ask for anyone's help within this issue.

She had to find Emma as she was the only one who knew of the issue and the only one who it was safe to discuss this with. It was just being able to find the right time and place to discuss it with her. Amy knew that there were cameras and microphones everywhere, so she needed to think carefully about where she was going to have this conversation. She needed to think about this carefully as the importance of this conversation had never been more important.

Amy quickly finished her tea and jumped in the car. She had to get out of the house and sort this. She had to go and speak to Emma. She had sort this out with her. Amy drove down to the alley where they met and found her phone, she sent her a text:

'I need to see you NOW, meet me in the usual place so we can have a chat'

Amy knew she would come as soon as she saw it. She had tried to make it look urgent without making Emma worry when she saw it. It was difficult when they were both partnered off with other men when really, they wanted to be together and to be living their life together. This type of lifestyle was not working for them, but it was the law. And now they had been found out and they had to decide how they were going to deal with this and how they were going to go forward.

It felt like hours before she replied. It did not feel like the few minutes that it actually was. Amy felt like she had waited an eternity for her to reply.

'I will be there in 10, just let me chat to the boy and I will be with you x'

The fact that she called him the boy made Amy chuckle, it makes them sound like some strange creature that she was caring for. Which, to be fair, they were. It was only Emma who could make her smile in this situation, another reason why Amy loved her.

Chapter 7

Amy sat in her car waiting until she saw the lights come round the corner. She could not control her heartbeat, it felt like it was going at one hundred times a minute. She had no idea what to do, she could only hope that Emma would have some magical solution that would allow them to live their lives together and free from the laws of this stupid place. She was hoping that Emma would be able to solve all the problems. As she sat their waiting, for what felt like an eternity, Amy's mind began to wander into the realms of what if.

She began to imagine what it would look like when her and Emma were stood at the hanging stage and were being hanged side by side in front of the whole village. What would be worse was that the all the people would be out there to watch them being hanged and would be informed of their crime. This meant, more than anything, that Amy's parents would be informed, and she knew that they would be disappointed. They wouldn't know what to do. This was not something that Amy had thought about until now.

She had not even thought about informing her parents of what she was going through. Her father would definitely not understand due to his monitor upbringing and the fact that he loved the rules, but her mother might just understand. Her mother might just be able to understand what was happening within Amy's life and that gave Amy a lot of comfort to think that her mother would understand.

Emma's car came into view and put an abrupt stop to Amy's wandering mind. She had to sort something out tonight as she would have to report something to the boss tomorrow when she went into the office as he would want to know what she had done towards the investigation in the time that she had not been in the office. Amy only hoped that Emma would be able to think of something as her brain had been completely blank because of sheer panic.

Emma jumped out of her car and into Amy's, she could tell by the way that Amy had worded her text message that something serious had gone on and she was curious and worried as to what was happening within their lives that had caused the sudden panic with Amy. She got into the car quickly, but in such a way that almost told Amy that she was not worried. Emma had put across this great image of calm and it spread across them both like wildfire.

"So, what's up? You sounded desperate in the message, so I came straight here? Is everything okay?"

Amy did not know how to respond. She did not know how to give her the information that she had gained from the boss this morning. How was she going to give such bad news to her best friend and the woman that she loved? How was she going to inflict this panic on the love of her life? Amy thought for a while before she began speaking.

She had to make sure that she was honest, but that she did not give out too much detail and throw the whole investigation. She needed to tell Emma the details that she needed but she could not tell her anymore. She had to keep some authenticity when it came to her job, otherwise all that training had been for nothing. She had to stick to her code of conduct but still Emma what was happening. After thinking for a while, Amy knew that she could do that.

She turned to face Emma and grabbed her hand. She had to be honest with her. She had to tell her what was happening. She could do this. They had to sort out a solution to this problem as she would have to report something in the morning regarding what she had done to help improve the situation.

"Babe, we need to sort something out. Someone has reported homosexual behaviour to my boss, and he has assigned me the task of discovering who the offenders are so that he can hang them in the square. It's the first time that hanging has been accepted with such feedback. It was like the whole office couldn't wait until they could see the offenders being hanged."

"It was scary. It's like homosexuals are the only ones who deserve to be hanged. Breaking the law is something that doesn't happen here and now it has happened it's like the people can't wait until the hanging happens and they can watch it. We need to do something as I need to report something in the morning to the boss and I just don't know what to do."

Amy had broken down while explaining to Emma. She did not realise but she had managed to curl up on Emma's lap during her speech and did not know how she had got there. She did not know what else to say, she could only hope that Emma had some cunning plan that was going to make all the problems go away and allow them to live their happy lives within their home community.

Homosexual behaviour should not be banned, and she hoped that Emma had a way of making it legal. This was obviously impossible but there had to be some way that they could live their lives together happily and legally without the risk of being hanged only around the corner. There had to be some sort of solution to the problem that they could find. There just had to be.

Emma sat there for a while thinking about what she had just been told. The distress on her face was clear, but it was clear that she was sat thinking now and not worrying in the way that Amy had when she was talking. Emma sat still and did not say a word, she simply sat. Amy was composing herself while Emma was thinking and was sitting eagerly waiting for her response. The tension in the car was rising. Both girls did not know what to say to each other. They were stuck. There was no answer to this question. No answer that would benefit anybody. But there had to be. There had to be some way they could be together.

"What if, and I know you're going to say that I am crazy and that there is no way that we could do this, but what if we ran away to America. I know that the fence is protected all the time and I know that there is the actual fence that we would have to compete with. But what if there was a way out and we could carry on and live our lives. What if somehow, we managed it."

"We could live truly together and be a normal family. There would be no hiding or worrying or just generally stressing. It would all be accepted for what it is, true love. We wouldn't have to worry about what other people would say or who we told as it is widely accepted over there. No one is getting hanged for being gay within America. We just have to find a way to get past the fence undetected. I reckon we could sort a way."

Amy didn't know what to say. Emma's idea was slightly crazy, but the more Amy thought about it the more it made sense. They could get over to America and live like their true selves. They wouldn't have to worry about what other people would say if they saw them. They wouldn't have to be careful where they met. They could live together happily, and no one would bother them. They could live a happy life.

This was all possible and it was in the future, Amy just had to find a way that would allow them to get past that fence. She was in the best position to do this as she was higher within the monitor class to allow her to see the rotations of people on watch at the fence. Amy sat thinking for a while as to when she could investigate the rotations and how she would be able to gain this information.

She sat and thought for a while and Emma just waited patiently for her to come back to the conversation. She had no idea what she was thinking but Emma would wait until she had thought of something as her ideas were usually good ones. They just took a long time to form. Emma was used to this and waited patiently before Amy spoke.

Amy suddenly looked like she had concluded her thoughts, her brain lighted up with her idea.

"Okay, I have an idea, but we will have to share this with Max for the plan to go through. So, Max works within the fence department where they work on who is watching the fence and who comes too near the fence. This means that he will be able to investigate the system and know when the rotations happen. This will allow us to have a time as to when it would be safe to try and get under the fence."

"I was also wondering if he could try and do the shift himself and then he would be able to not report us to the boss. This would obviously only work if the cameras were not working for some reason so we would have to think of a way to get rid of the cameras before we tried to carry out this plan. But it is achievable, I think. I might have just made it sound a lot easier than it is. What do you think?"

You could see on Emma's face that she had no idea what to say. Her life was hanging in the balance and her only options right now were to either carry on with her pretend life that she was trying to live, or she could carry out Amy's plan and live her true life with her true love. She knew what she wanted in the end, but the journey to get there seemed impossible at this moment. She didn't want Amy's partner to know as this was another person who would be able to tell someone and their whole lives would be over.

Amy waited for Emma's reply, she wanted her to agree so badly, but then at the same time was concerned about what her parents would think. She didn't want them to find out how she had developed such feelings for a woman or how she had completely ignored their rules and carried on like this behind their back. She didn't want to have to leave her life behind and everyone she loved. It would mean that she would have to give up everything she had for Emma.

This was something she was willing to do, she would do anything for Emma, but it would be the actual doing it, that would hurt. She couldn't even imagine life without her parents, but this was something that she was going to have to deal with if she wanted to live the rest of her life with Emma. She was going to have to start a completely new life in America and try and start all over again.

They were both going to have to find jobs and try and figure out what they could do within the real world, as there would be no monitor jobs in America.

Amy could see that Emma was thinking it through. She was unsure. That much was clear, and the more Amy thought about it she could understand why. How would this plan work in the grand scheme of it all? Would this be possible? Could they make this work? Emma was thinking it through and thinking about what she could say about this.

The emotions on Emma's face were clear. As she slowly concluded she began to speak. She started slowly but become more confident as she spoke.

"Okay, let's give it go, I think we would be better off in America and it's not like there is anything holding us back here, really. I mean we have our families but that is honestly all we have. I do think this is the best thing for us."

Emma looked unsure; you could see it on her face. But it was clear that she did want to do it. She knew that it would be hard, but it was something that had to be done. They could not stay there and wait until they had been found out and then be hanged. They had to work together and find a way to get themselves out of this situation. They could not carry on like this.

They had two very simple choices. Either stay there and severe ties with each other completely and vow to never speak to each other again or move to America and live the life that they had been dreaming about since college. They could not carry on with this life, it was just not possible. They could not just forget about each other and hope that everything would be okay, it just wouldn't happen. They had to be together. There was no other way for them to live their lives. They just had to be together.

Both girls sat waiting for something to happen, for something to come and give them a sign as to what they had to do and how they could do it. It didn't happen, as expected. Amy was the first to move, as she was the one who was the first to think of the next step.

"Right, I'll speak to Max tonight and see what he has to say about it. I honestly think he will be okay with it all. I'm sure he knows part of it anyway, so I don't think it's going to be a big shock for him. He must know something is going on, most of my friends have children on the way by now and me and him have only just started to get on like friends, so surely, he must know."

Emma sat listening, Amy could tell that she was thinking. She didn't want to tell Max as it meant involving another person in this mess of a situation. It meant having someone else to rely on and someone else to keep the secret and hope that they don't say anything. This was a big ask, and it was something that Emma was very scared of. She didn't want to involve someone who didn't need to know as it made the possibility of being found out that much more likely.

It made the chance of being hanged so much more real. She didn't know Max as well as Amy did and she did not know if he could be trusted. How was she supposed to know if he could be trusted? She knew that she trusted Amy. So, right now, she knew that that would have to be enough. If Amy thought that Max could be trusted, then Emma would agree with her. There was no other option really. They would have to trust him if this plan was to work out. It was the only way that the plan could ever work. They would not be able to work the plan without the help of Max. They had to involve him.

After mulling it over, Emma decided that they would have to include Max within their decisions. That was their only option. If they were planning on running away from Baskerville, they were going to have to get through the fence and there would be no better option than having a fence monitor on their side.

"Okay, I think you're right. We need some sort of back up and I think Max probably is the best bet. This is the best idea. Well, it's our only idea but it's better than nothing, we'll just have to make sure that we can trust Max as much as you say we can, because I don't want to give him all this information and then allow him to screw us over, because if that happens, we are screwed, completely. We have to make sure we can trust him completely before we tell him anything."

Amy knew what Emma was afraid of, but she had a better understanding of Max than Emma did, and Amy knew that she could trust Max. She just needed to see if he would help. That was the problem, Amy knew that she could trust him and that he wouldn't tell anyone, but it would be the encouraging him to help that would be the issue.

It was a big ask, asking someone to put their whole career and possibly their life on the line to help them to escape and then leave him to then deal with the consequences when they had left. Amy would have to speak to Max soon. She wanted to get this plan in action as soon as she could, now they had spoken about it, it had to happen.

Amy looked at Emma, she could see that she was worried, but she had to get this plan into action. Now it had been spoken about she had to make it happen.

"Don't worry, I will speak to Max tonight and see if we can get this plan into action. We need to get this moving and see if we can get out of this hell hole of a place. We need to start our life; we need to see if we can make this work, but we need to get out of here first."

Emma was worried, she didn't trust Max as much as Amy did and she didn't know how she was going to deal with letting someone in on their secret. She didn't know if Max would help them to get out, she was worried that he would report them and leave them in prison rotting before being hanged. There was just so much that could go wrong with bringing someone into this problem.

"Amy, we don't have to do this, it was just an idea. It was just with you saying how fed up you were of it here and how you couldn't carry on. It was just me throwing an idea around. If you don't think that we can trust Max, then we just don't do it. I shouldn't have put that pressure on you. I'm sorry."

Emma didn't know what to do. She had brought up her idea more as a joke than anything else, but the more that the girls had talked about it, the more it had become a reality. The more it had seemed as though it could work. They could escape this place and maybe they could be together properly. It was just a talk of a plan; it was nothing yet. But Emma could see the anxiety rising in Amy in a way that she had never seen before.

She did not want to cause any more stress for her that was unnecessary. She knew that this plan would be stressful for all of those involved. But it was something that she was going to have to be a part of now that they had been teased. This idea was like a carrot on a string, and both girls wanted nothing more than to grab that carrot with both hands and have it for themselves. They had to make this plan a reality. It was the only way.

Amy trusted Max, but there was that one part of her that thought he might resent her when he finally found out. He might take back everything that he had said. Max was happy with their relationship, but he did not know the whole story. He simply knew that Amy did not want to be with him, he did not know that she was already in love with someone. This was a problem that did not happen within Baskerville. You were partnered with the person you were given and that was it, no discussions. The idea of being someone who had not been assigned to you was unheard of. If it ever did happen, it was not discussed. This was what made Amy nervous. This was new territory; it was unheard of.

How would Max react when she told him? This was a massive gamble that she had to take if this plan was going to succeed. The reality was they could not do it without him. She had to think of a way of making this happen without telling Max too much, but it was not possible. She would have to come clean completely to him and simply hope that he understood. She would tell him and judge his reaction before she brought Emma into it. This could be the end of her life if Max did not agree with what she was saying. It could be the end of everything, if she did not do this correctly.

"I'll tell Max, I'll tell him how I am feeling but I will not mention your name. Until I can judge his reaction and see what he is going to do, I will not bring your name into this. If one of us goes down for this, it should be me. It was me who started it, and I'll finish it if I must. But we have to do something. I'll tell Max and if it ends up with me on the stage then at least I have tried."

Amy had made her decision and there was nothing that could be said that would stop her now. Her decisions were final, and Emma knew that, so she knew better than to argue with her at this point. Both girls looked at each other with a little fear and a little excitement. There was a small chance that they would be able to escape this madness. It was only a very small chance, but it was bigger than it had been when the day had started and both girls saw this as a positive.

Emma gave Amy a kiss on the cheek and told her that everything was going to be okay and walked away. She knew that she could trust Amy with anything so that was all she needed.

Both girls said goodbye and decided that Amy should speak to Max tonight while all of it was fresh in her mind. She needed to persuade Max to help them to get out, she needed to get him to understand why this had to happen.

Amy jumped in the car and drove home; she was thinking about how she was going to bring it up in conversation and how she was going to tell him. She figured he already had some sort of idea that there was something going on because they had only been living together like friends rather than like a married couple.

He had to know that there was something going on outside their relationship. But actually telling him would be really hard, informing him of all the things that she had been doing behind his back, that would make the whole thing worse. He was currently sat thinking that his life was all sorted and that soon we would be thinking about having children, and Amy was there about to tell him that this was all a lie.

Amy got home and got out of the car, she had a small chat with herself and went into the house. She had to have this chat with Max and see if he was onboard to help them to escape.

It was a conversation that could not be escaped from. If she was going to do this, she was doing it now. There was no other option. She would have to think about how to approach the subject with him and how to bring it up, but that was something she could do within the conversation. For now, she could only hope that he would understand and that he would fully empathise with her and what was happening. But the most important thing and the only way this plan could go ahead was if he agreed not to tell anybody.

Amy was aware that Max was high up in the monitors. Just like she was. He would have the ability to have her hanged in minutes. He may have been the person that she had been partnered with, but he was also the person that was being robbed of a life. Amy begged internally that he would help her, but the only way that he could help her was if she asked for the help, and that was going to be hard enough in itself.

Chapter 8

Amy didn't know how to start the conversation. She knew that she was going to crush all his dreams for the future. She knew that this would be the end of anything that they may have built together. But it was something that she had to do. She needed his help, and this was the only way to get it.

She sat down at the table, as he had made tea that night, another reason why she felt so bad. He really was the perfect guy. If only she could carry on with life in the normal way. The way that was expected of her. She would be happy. He nearly always made tea and made sure that Amy was happy. He truly had devoted his whole life to ensuring that Amy was happy, and she was about to throw all of that away and run away, while leaving Max to clean up the mess that she had left behind. This really was a selfish act. But it was a selfish act that had to be done if Amy and Emma would ever be happy together.

Max had dished out the tea with a glass of wine to complement the food perfectly. Amy was building up her courage to say something. Over dinner was the best time to do this. It was a time when there were no other distractions and Max would have to listen to her. Amy built up the courage inside herself. She could tell that Max knew something was up as he kept checking in on her, but Amy could not say anything until she had built up the courage inside herself.

"Max, I have to speak to you about something. It is going to come as quite a shock, but I want you to sit and listen to what I am going to say. Once I have told you all this, I am then going to ask for your help, you don't have to help me obviously, but it would be so appreciated if you would."

Max looked at Amy unable to find the words to explain how he was feeling. He did not know how to tell Amy how he felt, he knew there was something not quite right with their relationship. He knew how he felt towards Amy, but he had known for a long time that all these feelings were not reciprocated. It was just something that he would have to live with. He could never have prepared himself for what Amy was about to tell him though. This secret was something that only appears within Baskerville every 100 years or so and something of this nature had not appeared before.

"Max, you have probably noticed that me and you have not been together in the way that we are supposed to be, and I am sure that you are beginning to wonder why. The honest answer is that I am in love with someone else. I have been in love with them since we were in monitor college together. It is just something that I cannot ignore, and I cannot live my life without them. I am truly sorry, and I cannot imagine what you are going through right now. I am sorry that I have had to tell you like this and at this time, I wish more than anything it could have worked out differently for us, but it just hasn't and for that I am sorry."

Max sat for a moment and took in what he had just been told. He seemed quite composed considering what he had just been informed and he didn't seem to be angry, which is what Amy was most worried about.

"Amy, I have known since the moment you walked through that door that we would never be together the way that we are meant to be. I could tell that your heart belonged to someone else. It is not something to be ashamed of. It is just a shame that within Baskerville this is something that cannot be acted upon. I just have one question to ask, who is he?"

That was when it hit Amy, Max thought that all this time she had been hiding away with another man. It did make sense as she thought about it further. Homosexual activity would be the last thing on Max's mind. It was not something that occurred within most lifetimes never mind to your own partner. She had to be careful how she told him the next part of the story as he could become offended and inform the authorities.

"Max this is the thing, there would not have been a problem if it was a man. If I wanted a man our relationship would be perfect, you are so lovely, and I could not imagine living with another man. But this is the problem I am not in love with a man I'm in love with a woman. Before I go any further within my explanation, I need to know that you are not going to tell anyone. I do not want her to be hanged. They can hang me, but they are not going to hang her."

Amy stopped; she didn't want to go any further with her explanation until she was sure that Max was trustworthy. She waited for his response. This was the moment, the moment when it could go either really well or terribly wrong. Amy did not like having such a large decision put into the hands of someone else.

She was beginning to regret this idea. She could see Max processing the information, but she was worried about the outcome. If he decided to tell someone, her whole life would be in tatters. She did not know what to do. She sat and allowed Max time to come to terms with what she had just said. She could feel her heart rate quickening, she had given this man a chance to completely ruin her life and she was beginning to regret it.

Max looked bewildered; he did not know what to say. It took a few moments for what had just been said to fully kick in. He knew that there was something not quite right within his love life with Amy, but he had never suspected it was something of this scale. He didn't know what to say, he knew that even from hearing what he had just been told, he was now breaking the law by not phoning to monitors immediately.

This was a big thing to put on a person, a big responsibility how did she know that he wasn't about to tip off the monitors and get her hanged. This was what changed his mind. Even though their relationship had not gone as they should have done, she trusted him enough to inform him of her difficult situation. This was the defining factor that swayed him, she trusted him, and no one can put a price on trust.

"Amy the thing with love, is that we can't choose it, it chooses us. It is just unfortunate that who you have been chosen to love puts you in a very difficult position. You know it is illegal for this to ever happen? If someone finds out, you will both be hanged no matter what excuses you throw at them. I do hope you have a plan, because you cannot just carry on hiding this as someone is bound to find out. This is not a secret that can be kept, it will eventually come out and then you will be dead. What did you need my help with, just tell me and I'll do it?"

Max's readiness to assist was another reason why Amy was so grateful to have Max by her side. Had all this craziness not begun she would have been so happy with Max, and they would have lived a great life together. It just wasn't supposed to be that way. As Max said, we don't choose who we love, love chooses us. This sentiment was something that had resonated with Amy, it made her feel as though all of this wasn't her fault, she wasn't to blame. It was quite comforting.

Amy knew she was going to have to confine in him now and tell him the plan. She couldn't ask for his help without telling him the plan, it was just whether he was going to tell the monitors or risk his life for her. At this moment, she could not be sure, why would he? Why would anyone put their life on the line for someone who they barely even know who had already ruined their lives?

Amy took a deep breath and began explaining her plan to Max, she went into great detail about what he would have to do and how his role was crucial to the whole operation going ahead smoothly. She also went into detail about how she would be getting over the fence with Emma – not mentioning her name of course as this was too risky at this point. When Amy had finished, she sat back down and waited. She was aware that she had given him a lot to think about and she knew he would need some time before he answered.

As the silence drew on, Amy began to think that the plan was insane. How could she believe that she would be able to escape this crazy place? Surely people had tried before, but no one had ever escaped, that was the thing. It had never happened. The silence was killing Amy from the inside out, the self-doubt that was filling her skull, it felt like it was eating her alive. She was unaware of it, but she had begun to shake uncontrollably as she sat at the table. Her whole life was in the hands of a man she barely knew. This was not a position Amy enjoyed being in.

Chapter 9

Sitting home alone was not where Emma wanted to be when her whole life was on the line. She trusted Amy with her life, and she knew that she would not do something that would put her in danger, but it wasn't Amy that Emma was worried about. Amy's natural defence strategy would have kicked in and she would not have mentioned Emma's name, but what if Max was not as trustworthy as Amy made out, what if tomorrow Amy was being hanged. If that happened Emma did not know what she would do, it was likely she would confess and hang there too, with her one true love.

One million thoughts were rushing through her head. How did she manage all these thoughts, all these possible scenarios that could happen? Without thinking she grabbed her car keys and started her car. She knew where she was going, she knew it wasn't right, but it was something that had to be done. She had to know what was happening to her life. She had to know if Max had told the monitors or if he was willing to help. She couldn't sit in the house and wonder any longer.

It was a long drive to Amy's house. It was almost like their houses had been placed at the furthest point away from each other deliberately. This was simply speculation, but Emma felt like everyone was watching her drive to the other side of town, wondering what she was doing. She did not care though. She had to be there. She had to know what was happening to her life.

All through the drive Emma started to notice the number of cameras that were on the roads of Baskerville. It was something she had never taken any notice of until now. As she drove along the road, she began to notice them all at consistent intervals within the road. She presumed these were to monitor the traffic that drove along the roads and to see how many people were using them. The traffic cameras were not in her job section.

These were down to the traffic monitors, so Emma had rarely seen them. She wondered if she was being watched right now through them and if people were wondering where she was going and why she was going there. At this point, Emma did not care. She just knew that she had to know how the conversation had gone with Max and if she needed to prepare for freedom or death. But the more Emma thought about it. They were both the same thing at the end of the day.

As Emma reached the house, she noticed how nice it was at this end of town. She noticed how different it was to her house. Amy really had done well for herself within monitor school, the higher grades had meant that she was straight into the higher department and gained the better house and car. As Emma had not done that great, she was awarded with living in the slightly less attractive part of town. Although she got the most work in this area, she did often wonder what it would be like to live here.

Emma jumped out of the car and walked into the house; she didn't even knock. She was so caught up in the panic that knocking on the door seemed pointless at this moment. She walked down the long hallway and into the kitchen where she presumed Amy and Max would be, as she opened the kitchen door, she saw Amy passed out on the floor, she couldn't understand what had happened and rushed over to her.

"Amy, talk to me, come on you have to wake up babe, you have to tell me what happened."

Emma had not even thought about Max, he was stood there simply watching. Taken back by what had just happened. He did not know where to put himself. He only knew that in this room was a stranger, his wife and himself and it seemed that he was the odd one out.

"Amy, please you can't leave me like this, I need you. Please wake up baby, we have things we need to do!"

Amy stirred, Emma jumped off her and gave her some space, she didn't know what to do. Amy opened her eyes and grabbed hold of Emma so tightly it was like she would never let go. Both girls were entangled in each other when Emma kissed her. It was the deepest kiss that Amy had ever had, the desperation could be felt within it, the need, and the cruelty of this society. Amy kissed her back, so grateful to see her. It was moments like this that it was clear that the girls were meant for each other, the way they fitted together; It just worked.

This kiss was the most intense kiss either girl had ever experienced. This was love, true love. Even though there was no doubt in either girl's mind, the kiss only confirmed it. There was no one in this world that would break them apart.

Emma began to cry as she was kissing Amy and threw all her emotions into the kiss Amy grabbed her in a protective way that calmed Emma and helped her to understand that Amy would always be there to protect her. Both girls pulled out of the kiss simultaneously and finished with a shorter kiss that still had all the meaning. Then they sat, looking at each other and wondering what they were going to do.

Both girls suddenly remembered, almost at the same time, that they had an audience. Max's presence had been forgotten about in the panic of Amy passing out. They both stopped at once and looked at him. Max was standing there simply watching. He had a confused look on his face, but Amy perceived this as processing. This was the moment where Max would decide, Amy could feel it. Seeing them together would either make him want to help or make him call the monitors. It was all in this moment, their lives hung by a thread. Max took what seemed to be forever before he spoke. Both girls looking at him, their desperation showing in their eyes. Max knew what he was going to do, he just wasn't sure how he was going to get away with it.

"So, I'm guessing this is the girl? The girl that you want to risk it all for? I can see how much she means to you Amy and your relationship is everything I wanted us to have. That real connection. When you have that someone, it is not something that should be thrown away. It should be cherished and kept safe."

Amy was beginning to relax. Max's opening speech had allowed her to relax slightly as he was making a good case as to why they should be together, so this filled her with the hope that he was going to help them. This allowed her to imagine her life away from Baskerville and in a place where she could be herself. Emma grabbed her hand seeking comfort, Amy squeezed it tighter as Max carried on.

"I want to help you; I feel I owe it to you. I honestly think that the plan has some good points within it. There are a few moments where I would change a few things, but I think we can do this. I will just have to edit the time sheet slightly and accidentally break a few cameras and then it should be plain sailing. I want to do this for you both. You need to get out of here, and the only way you're going to do that is getting over that fence."

Both girls pulled Max into an embrace. They could not believe it. He was going to help. All those moments of worrying that he was going to tell the monitors, worrying that he wouldn't help. They had all been for nothing. Amy knew that there was good in him, which was why she had asked him. She just wasn't sure how far that good would stretch. Putting his life on the line for them was a massive ask, but he had agreed. This was it. They were going to get out of here.

The trio finished off the bottle of wine in celebration and talked through the logistics of the plan, thinking about how it would work and the problems that they might encounter. Before they realised, it was midnight and they decided they all needed some sleep.

"Amy, you take the bed, I'll sleep down here – I think you two should be together tonight."

Amy didn't know what to say, she truly had been assigned the nicest man in Baskerville. Had this all turned out differently she was sure that she would have been so happy with him, she was almost sad that things had worked out this way.

"Max, you truly are a gentleman – come on Emma you need your sleep."

Chapter 10

Both girls were charged, they were excited they were going to get out of this hell hole and live to tell the tale. They had been gifted this night together, and neither of them was ready to waste it.

"This feels almost normal."

Emma was laid in bed watching Amy undress. This was something they had not done in a long time. They had not been together in a room since that night before graduation. It had always been done in secret – usually in a car, parked down a dark alley. This actually felt like they could be a couple a normal couple. Amy knew this was meant to be. She could not imagine being with anyone else now. Emma had got under her skin. She got into bed and as Emma cuddled into her, she knew that she would never let any harm come to this woman.

"I love you, and I think I always will."

Amy did not know where those words had come from, but she felt as though someone needed to say it.

These words brought out the other side of Emma, she turned from her anxious and worried self into the cheeky and confident woman that Amy had fallen in love with. She jumped on top of Amy and began to emulate the kiss that they had experienced in the kitchen. This kiss was better though. Instead of the desperation and fear, this was filled with hope and excitement. Emma was taken over by an instinct and Amy could have peaked simply from that kiss alone but before Amy had time to kiss her back Emma had moved on, she slowly worked her way down to Amy's breasts and was kissing and playing with them until Amy's nipples were standing to attention.

Amy could feel the warmth flowing already but she knew that she must hold on. How did this girl do this to her? Emma was running her hands gently between Amy's thighs only to find that Amy was ready for her. Emma started to kiss her again, while her fingers danced on Amy's point creating a rhythm that was so otherworldly, Amy began to moan. Emma knew that Amy was close and slowly inserted two fingers inside her. Once she was inside, Amy's voice told her all she needed to know – she was close.

"How do you do this to me? Oh my god—yes—oh yes—keep going—I love you so much!"

Emma relished in Amy's words; she knew they were all genuine even if they were uttered at a time when a woman would say anything. Gently moving her fingers around insider her Emma began to feel Amy clamping around her. Amy began bucking uncontrollably and screaming – once Amy let go, a rush of excitement filled both girls. Amy went limp underneath Emma who looked at her with so much love that their relationship could never be doubted.

Emma rolled over, proud of what she had just accomplished. She was fuelled by the idea of being free of this place very soon. Her dream of being with Amy in a way normal couples were together was becoming a reality.

Both girls lay staring at each other for hours. They did not want to go to sleep. They had a fear of waking up and their partner being gone. They were in this together and nothing was going to allow them to fall apart.

Amy grabbed Emma's hand and kissed it slowly – Emma knew where this was going to go and pulled her towards her mouth eagerly.

"I can't actually believe we are having to hide like this. The country should be happy that there is true love in the world. They shouldn't be angry that we are breaking the rules. I just don't understand this world it is so odd."

Emma knew that Amy could get philosophical when she was aroused but she didn't have the time for it right now. Emma wanted Amy so badly that she did not want to hear her putting the world to rights even though at times that was something so sexy that Emma could not control herself. She wasn't in the mood to listen to her argue about things that she could not change. She was ready to escape and change her world, but she was not convinced that they could change the world as a whole.

Emma grabbed Amy and threw her on top of her. She kissed her so hard that Amy could not carry on with her rant. This seemed to refocus Amy as she remembered what she had set out to do. She ran her fingers along Emma's back and grabbed and pulled her closer. No one could kiss like Amy. She had a skill that allowed you to think that you were being sucked into her completely it was distracting. It was a kiss that made you forget everything. It was a kiss that meant no matter was happening on the outside world within that kiss you would be fine.

Emma was deepened in the kiss and wanted to only go deeper in when Amy broke off. She began to work down Emma's body exploring all of her with her hands. Just her simple touch was beginning to work to Emma – she could feel the familiar warmth rushing to her middle. She could not understand how one woman could be so captivating but here she was merely kissing her, and Emma could feel the explosion coming far too soon. She knew that she couldn't suppress it she had tried to too many times to make the moments last longer, but it was a battle she would never win.

Amy was like a woman on a mission, she quickly moved from Emma's middle down towards her thighs. She stroked them up and down with the lightest touch – this magical feeling made Emma moan. Emma could feel that she was close, but she had to hold on, she had to let Amy know how she felt at the right time, she could not let go yet. Amy knelt down and it as very clear where she was headed. Her kisses were travelling downwards, and Emma was lit up with excitement. This was going to be incredible!

Amy slowly worked her way down to Emma's point and as she did, she began to play with her clit with her tongue. The feeling sent shivers down Emma's spine. She had never felt like this before. Amy was kissing and sucking and doing everything in her power to make Emma feel good. Emma began bucking uncontrollably under her and Amy knew that she was close. She slowly inserted two fingers insider her – knowing that this would begin something. As she went in, she could feel that Emma was ready. She had never been wetter in the whole time they had been dating.

Amy knew that this time it was different, she knew that this time she had done well. Emma was holding on, but she could not hold on for much longer. She was going to have to let go soon and when she did Emma could feel that it was going to be mind-blowing. Amy carried on working her mouth and created a rhythm for Emma to follow as she inserted her fingers in the same rhythm, she could feel Emma tense around her, and Amy knew that she was close. When Emma came, it was a wave of emotion, as she collapsed around Amy, Amy grabbed her and pulled her into the most intense kiss that she had ever had. Both girls collapsed onto the bed and led there together.

Chapter 11

BANG!

Both girls awoke with a start, what was that noise? They looked at each other in sheer panic. That kind of bang at this time in the morning could have only been someone knocking the door down, and there were only certain people who were allowed to knock a door down in the middle of the night and they can only do it if they have good reason.

"Emma, baby, you need to wake up! This is important come on get up get dressed!"

Amy didn't mean to shout but the adrenaline was getting the better of her. All this time and their life was about to come crumbling down. She had to get Emma out of the house. Having someone to stay without the correct paperwork was suicide, without adding the threat of homosexual activity which was plain for anyone to see.

Amy didn't know how she was going to get out of this one, she would have to ride it out and see where it took her. But she knew for one thing. If she was going down, she was not taking Emma with her.

"Amy, we know you're in there so it would be better for everyone if you just let us in. We just need to speak to you that is all. There have been reports that there is someone in your apartment who is not a resident and we need to talk about this. You know the rules – no one round after curfew."

Emma was shaking, she knew the person was her and she didn't know how she was going to explain herself out of this one. She quickly put on her clothes and went out the door, both girls walked out and sat at the table like robots. They knew the drill they had been here many times before it was just, they were usually the ones doing the interview not the ones that were being interviewed.

Amy knew that this didn't happen unless there was solid evidence that wrongdoing had happened. They probably had all the evidence they needed to string them both up, but Amy was going to fight this. She had to. There was no way she was seeing the love of her life being hanged purely because of who she loved. It was not something she could bare to see. It was something she had to fight.

"So, do you have an explanation for what is going on here Amy? Emma should not be here; it is hours past curfew what is going on?"

Amy sat and thought for a moment. She wasn't sure whether to just come clean there and then and see if she could appeal but she knew that this was not going to end well either way, so she may as well try to act innocent.

"Emma is having trouble at home and she occasionally comes here for a break from her partner. They really don't get on and it is becoming difficult for her to live with him, so she comes here for a break. Things just got a little out of hand tonight, so she stayed longer than expected. That's when Max offered to take the couch so that Emma could stay in the bed, and I wasn't about to sleep on the floor and as we've been friends since monitor school it is fine. Best friends share a bed all the time."

As soon as Amy said it, she knew that last line wasn't going to help her. She should have stopped at monitor school. The monitor looked at them thoroughly while he was deciding what to do with this evidence. Emma was quietly sitting in the background scared to even make a noise. Amy did not want her to go down as – well but Amy could not see this being a single prosecution. At the end of the day, she couldn't be gay on her own and it was very clear who she had been with.

"I think I should take you both down to headquarters for tonight and then we can interview you individually in the morning. I don't have the brain power for this now."

Amy knew there was no point fighting it. This was her career gone, her life gone and most importantly her love gone. She would never recover from this. Even if by some miracle she didn't get hanged she would have no job as she wouldn't be allowed back to monitor ranks after being held at headquarters.

As both girls were led into their cells Emma was crying. She knew what Amy knew. This was it. Neither of them could deny what the monitors had seen. It was very clear to anyone there what was happening within the house that night. It didn't take a genius to see that the two girls had been in the bed together and not in the cute slumber party sense that the girls were trying to pass it off as.

The cells were dank and dark. Once the lights had been switched off there was nothing. Everyone in there was silent. It was almost deathly. People say that death row in America was a scary place, but that has nothing on the headquarters at Baskerville. At least in America you get a trial. In Baskerville if the monitors say you had done it, then that was that. There wasn't even a public vote!

Amy slid down the fence and sat there. She had a feeling of emptiness within her that she knew would probably never be filled again. She knew this emptiness would fill her for the rest of her living days. As she sat there, she could hear Emma sobbing through the grates. This broke Amy's heart. Hearing the woman, you loved fear for her life. That was not a sound a woman wanted to hear again.

Chapter 12

Amy awoke with a start convinced that she had just had the strangest dream, as she reached over to wake Emma up, she realised that it had not been a dream. She really was stuck in the cells in the headquarters, her life really was on the line and Emma was sitting in her cell sobbing just as hard as she had been when Amy had fallen asleep.

Amy presumed it was morning now as there a faint glimpse lights rushing through the small window at the top of the cell. She hoped that they would interview them quickly and just get it over with, but she knew that people spent weeks, sometimes months in these cells.

To Amy's surprise she heard a bang at the end of the corridor. Could this be the moment of her interview? She had to think of something quick, how would she explain all this to the monitors?

The door on her cell was clanking. That only confirmed to Amy that the time had come for her to explain herself to the monitors and explain exactly what had been going on within that room. She had her story, and she was going to stick to it. She could not change her story now otherwise they would know that something was up. She had to follow the rules and hope that Emma did the same.

"Amy, you need to follow us down to the interrogation room. I need you to confirm your statement."

Amy had seen the interrogation room before when she was being shown around after she had been given the job of monitor. She knew what happened within that room and she knew that the monitors would do whatever they have to do in order to gain information. This was something that Amy did not want Emma to have to go through.

She was trying to think of a way of making a deal with them without making it painfully obvious what was happening between them. She wasn't sure if she could pass it on as purely friendship, not at this point in the interview. She knew that she was going to have to be convincing and would have to really convince them.

Amy had a million thoughts running her brain as she went into the room. The room was padded all the way around. The fences were padded in a sickening green padding that had a medical feeling. It was the kind of room that was like the torture chamber you imagine but with a clinical twist. There were hangings on the wall that held the tools. These tools were not your average back yard tools, these tools were designed for torture. They were designed to gain information and that was all.

They were purely there to cause pain, as much pain that could possibly be inflicted onto a human being without them dying. Amy had seen the demonstration and she knew that she was going to be on the end of these techniques if they did not believe her story. She knew that she was going to have to be convincing. But she knew that whatever they did to her she was not going to throw Emma under the bus. Whatever happened to her, she would do whatever she could to protect her girl.

"If you could just sit in this chair so we can strap you in."

Amy slowly lowered herself into the chair. She knew that she was being seated into the electric chair and she knew what happened within that chair. She was wincing before she even touched the chair. She knew what was about to happen and she knew how much it was going to hurt she just didn't know if she was going to be able to deal with it.

Even with the threat of the chair looming, Amy knew that she was not going to give up Emma. She knew that if she was able to give a convincing statement, they wouldn't question Emma. Amy had seen the interrogation room in action when she had first become a monitor, so she took this as an upper hand. She knew what tools they had to gain information and she knew how they would do it. This was something that most people within this room did not have.

She knew what was coming and she was prepared. No matter what they put her through she would not be giving up any information. She would not be giving up Emma. She just had to stay calm and stick to the story. If she stuck to the story with no holes within it, they would have no choice but to believe her. This was the only way that they were going to get out of this alive. She had to play the game, the game that the monitors had control of, but she was a monitor, and she wasn't going to let them forget that.

Once she was strapped into the chair, Amy sat and stared at the interviewer that was sitting opposite her. He had a control panel in his hand that controlled the chair and the amount of electricity that would be pounding through Amy's body at any moment now. Amy did not let this affect her. She was too strong for this. They wouldn't put too much through her otherwise she would die and they wouldn't want a death within the torture chamber that would be something that would cost the interviewer his job and Amy was aware of that.

"So, Amy, do you want to tell us what was happening within your house when the monitors entered."

Amy took a deep breath and began telling her story. She kept to the facts and did not wander from the story she thought through everything that she was saying and ensured that there were no holes within the story. The less questions that she had to answer meant that there would be less opportunity for the monitors to electrify her. They could only electrify her on the suspicion of a false answer, so this was something that she was not going to give them.

When Amy had finished her explanation, she could feel the sweat dripping from her forehead she could not let them see that they had rattled her. She took a deep breath and got her thoughts together. She could not allow these monitors to mess up what she had created. She was in love with this girl and she was not about to ruin her relationship purely because it was frowned upon by some men who claimed to rule the world.

When Amy had finished, the monitor looked her up and down reviewing what had just been said. The look on his face told Amy that he did not know whether to believe her or whether to use the chair. Amy was hoping for the first option, but she knew that it was very unlikely. The monitor was sat thinking and processing what had just been said to him. The suspense in the room was intolerable. The famous saying 'you could cut it with a knife' had never been more apt.

The monitor suddenly moved towards the control panel and Amy knew that the decision had been made, she could not move. She knew that soon the chair that she was sat in was going to send a thousand volts worth of electricity through her body. She was shaking but she could not show that to the monitor. He could not find out that she had been lying, he could not find out that this was all a lie. Amy made eye contact with the monitor and kept it while he pressed the button. Amy could never have prepared herself for the pain that came with the press of that button.

The electricity came into Amy's body like a wave. She could not cope with it. She could feel her body uncontrollably shaking with the volts of electricity that were being fired into her body. She could not control her body, it was doing what the electricity was telling it to do, she had no say in what it did.

It was like the electricity had taken over her body and her mind could not stop it. She just had to sit there and take the hit. She didn't have time to recover from the electricity before the monitor was firing questions at her again. She just had to keep to her story and hope that the motors believed her. She had run out of moves and the ball was completely in the monitor's court. Her whole life was in the hands of someone else and Amy could not deal with that.

"I will ask you again, now you know what happens when you lie to us, what was happening when the monitors walked into your house?" His voice had raised slightly and was beginning to show the anger that he was feeling. Amy saw this as an advantage, once the interviewer had lost his cool it showed that Amy had the upper hand. Once an interviewer had lost their temper it showed that the interviewee was winning.

"I have already told you what happened that night. Emma was staying at our place for the night as she is going through a lot at home so I said that she could come and stay at ours for dinner. We were sat chatting and drinking and then before we knew it, it was too late to go home, we had missed curfew. I know that missing curfew is a crime in itself and I will happily pay the fine for that but that is everything that happened that night.

Max said that Emma should have his space in the bed, and he would take the couch as he is a kind man and always believes that he should look after the girls. That is all that happened, once we had got into the bed that is when the monitors arrived. I don't know what you think you saw but this is not that. Emma and I are very good friends and we have been since monitor school, but there is nothing more between us. You can shock me all you like and keep doing it until I'm fried but I can't tell you something that is not true. The story is not going to change as this is the story and I cannot give you more than that."

Amy knew by looking at the monitor that he was considering her story. Because of how strong she had been within her statement the monitor was at a loss as to what to do with the interview. It was clear that he was not going to get anything from it now and there was no point in trying to go further with it.

"Okay, I will organise someone to take you home, but please be aware that you are on probation now and the monitors will be watching you closely. I should also tell you that you are no longer needed in the monitor department as it is a contrast of interest and you should not be able to know the works of the monitoring at this moment. Everyone in your office has been informed and told not to give you any information."

Amy felt only relief. The fact that she had lost her job was irrelevant she could not think about that right now. All she knew was that she was safe, and her life was going to carry on. She could only hope that she had done enough for them to not have to question Emma. She could only hope that was true.

As Amy walked through the corridor and past the cell that she had spent the night in, she looked onto Emma's cell next door and noticed that the door was open. She could only hope that this meant that Emma had been released. Amy hoped that she had been released and was not sitting in the chair that she had just been released out of.

"You are now free, but please remember about your probation, anything that happens to you we will know so try to follow the rules from now."

Amy looked at them and muttered under her breathe, she could not cope with the patronising monitors at this point she just wanted to get home and talk to Max. She would have to organise something with Emma to make sure that she was okay, but that could wait. Amy had to speak to Max and make sure that he was okay and that he was still up for the plan.

This encounter had only made Amy surer that she had to get out of this country. She had used up one of her lives and she did not know how many she had left. This was something that she did not want to learn. She did not want to be on that stage hanging from a rope. She would do anything to ensure that did not happen.

Chapter 13

Amy got into the car that had been provided and was hoping that none of the neighbours would be watching her get out of the car. People knew what the black cars were for and if the neighbours saw her get out of one of these, they would know that she had just been questioned. It was all part of the plan. Make the community aware of what was happening with the people around you. It was all part of the play. The monitors knew that with the neighbours watching her as well Amy would have to be even more careful than usual.

It was something that always seemed thought through and that they knew what they were doing. Amy hated them for it. She was going to have to see Emma at some point to give her the instructions for the plan, now that plan had been ruined. She would have to find a new way to get that information to Emma. Luckily, she was able to talk to Max freely, but would he be as willing now that he had seen first-hand the consequences of the actions that they were about to take on. Amy had so many questions running through her mind she did not know which one to answer first. But she knew one thing, this was going to be a lot harder now that the monitors were onto her.

Emma had been discharged and was sitting in her house when she saw the car drive past. She could see that Amy was sitting in the back and breathed a sigh of relief. She had been panicking that that was it for them, that they would have to answer more questions, get driven to a confession and then hung. She could not see another option at this point. It was the only way that this could go, but seeing Amy leaving in that car had given her some hope. It may not have been much, but it was hope and Emma was going to cling to whatever the world gave her, however small.

She just had to find a way to gain contact with Amy without the monitors finding out, she had to find out what the plan was, or if there even was one. They had to get out of this town and away from all these rules. Emma did not know how to gain a message. She was not as high up in the force as Amy and did not know the complete works of the monitor system. She was purely a spy. She found out information and gave it the officials, that was her job. She did not even know who she officially worked for, she just knew that she had to write everything up and upload it to the town document.

That was all that she was told. She was a first generation monitor so she was in the lowest of the ranks compared to Amy who was a second generation so she, naturally, was put further up the ranks instantly. She would have to get in touch with Amy somehow, but it was figuring out the best way to achieve this without the monitors finding out. She would have gone through Max but with the monitors knowing that there was something going on with him as well that channel was too risky. She would have to think of another way, there was just no other way. How was she going to get this information to Amy? She sat and thought but nothing was appearing, suddenly her phone pinged.

Emma jumped up quickly at the sound of her phone, she was so jumpy after spending a night in the cell. Nothing had happened to her and she hadn't even been interrogated, but she knew that Amy had. Just the idea of Amy being in that chamber, that she had been shown on her first day, was enough to make her afraid. She could not see a way out of this alive. Emma had already gone through all the potential outcomes of this text message before she opened her phone.

'Meet me at the bridge, 11pm. See you soon'

There was no sign off and Emma did not recognise the number, but she knew who it was from. It could only be from one person. The one person who Emma was ready to blow it all for.

Emma did not know what to do with this information. She quickly deleted the message. She knew full well that the monitors would be able to gain access to the message if they wanted to, but she felt like she had done something by deleting it. She would spend the rest of the day at home pretending that everything was fine, but when the time came. She would walk to the bridge, so that no one saw her car leave and then she would sort out this mess with the love of her life.

Amy could only hope that Emma would know who the message was from. She knew that using a non-regulation mobile was punishable by death but she was already so deep into another death penalty what difference would another make. She just needed to talk to Emma and ensure that she was okay. She needed to know that she was okay. Once she knew that she was okay she could then tell her the plan.

There was no plan yet, but that was her job for the rest of the day. She had a few hours to come up with something before she had to meet her, she would just have to make sure that Max was still up for the plan to take place. She had to get Emma out of this town, she had to ensure that Emma could be free. She was done caring about herself and ensuring that the two of them could live together, she just had to make sure that she was safe.

Time was running out for Amy to create a plan; she had been sitting staring at a blank piece of paper for hours before she had thought of anything. The original plan was not going to work with all the monitors watching her. The plan she had come up with was the only plan that she could think of. Stick to the original plan, but she did not take part in it. She would have to live out her days within Baskerville's fences and try to act happy. She was lucky, she got on with Max and she did think that she could live with him as friends and that Max would be happy with that. She just knew that it was not the same for Emma.

She had not been so fortunate with her partner and when it came to it Emma, would not be able to survive within these fences for much longer and Amy could not protect her forever. If Amy could get Emma out of this hell-hole, then she had a chance at living a normal life, being able to express herself freely and most importantly love who she wanted to love. Emma would get over Amy eventually and that was the only way that the two girls were going to survive. Amy knew that the monitors were keeping a closer eye on her and if she did not act soon both girls would be dead in a few days. If she could get Emma out, then maybe only one of them would have to die, but Amy was going to ensure it was not Emma.

Amy was sat on the dining table when she heard Max come home. She knew this was going to be a difficult conversation, but she also knew this was a conversation that she had to have with him. She had to sort this out and this conversation was the only way that she could do it.

"Max, can I speak to you about the plan. I feel like we might need to change it due to the circumstances. I don't even know if you are still up for carrying out the plan as it is putting your life at risk, but I need you, I can't do this without you. We need to ensure that Emma is safe. I don't care about me anymore I just need to get her to safety. I'm thinking of carrying out the same plan, but only getting Emma over the fence seems to be the best option."

Max paused for a second and thought about what he was going to say next. Amy had said her piece and had said all the information that he needed. She had not left out any details, she had told him her plan and had been very clear about her intentions. He just knew that he was stuck in the middle of this and did not know how to get out of it. In his mind, he was going to send both girls over the fence and be free of the drama, but it was becoming more and more clear that that was not going to be the case. He was going to be constantly stuck in this.

If Amy did not go across the fence with them, then he would be stuck in this turmoil for the rest of his life. He had to think of another way to control this, but he could not think of a way. Amy was right. If she left Baskerville the monitors would be onto them straight away, there would be no escape and he would be the one who would be left to take the blame. He could help both girls across the fence and solve all their problems, but that would lead to him probably taking the death penalty, but even if he just helped Emma then he would probably be stuck with the death penalty as well so there was no way that he was going to win.

His only other option would be to refuse. This was something that Max had been pondering for a while. He could refuse and say that he simply could not commit to that and risking his life, but that would lead to ruining his relationship with Amy. There was no good way out of this situation. He was in now, so he was going to have to get the girls out of it and deal with the consequences.

"I know what you are saying, and I do agree the monitors are going to be onto us 24/7 but we have to do something. We cannot have you two trying to live a lie for the rest of your lives. We have to do something. This is my way of showing of how much I care for you, I can't do what a partner should be able to do because of the situation that we are in, but I can do this for you. So let me, please."

Amy was taken aback. She did not know how to take this compliment. Max truly was the most amazing man that she had ever met. For her to be matched with him was one of the best things that had happened to her. Without Max, Amy would be unable to carry out the life that she wanted, she would be unable to carry out any of this plan that they had concocted together. Without Max she would be unable to run away to the life that she had only dreamed of because of the hell that she was living.

"I know that you are doing that thing where you slow everything down in your brain in order to take everything in, but I want you to know that I am with you, no matter what. I love you, as a friend, and I want you to be happy more than anything. This in-between that we are living in has to stop. We cannot carry on like this, I want you to be happy."

"If that means that I get hanged in the process, then that is the price that I am willing to pay. We need to get both of you out of here and I am going to help you do it. This is something that you have to do together. You cannot send Emma over that fence on her own. If you want to live together happily, then you have to go over the fence too. I understand the pressure that you are under, but this is something that you two have to do together."

This was the moment that Amy knew that she was looking at the kindest man she would ever meet. He truly was someone who could not be replaced. He was amazing.

Chapter 14

11 pm was approaching fast and Amy did not know how she was going to go through with the plan. She had to allow Emma to have a choice. She would be the deciding factor in all of this. Max wanted Amy and Emma to both go over the fence and be happy without him. Whereas Amy was thinking of sending Emma over by herself in order to ensure that Emma would be able to get to safety. This was something that she could not process on her own. She needed Emma to be able to put her opinion forward. She could not make a decision like this; it was affecting too many people's lives.

Amy came downstairs from the bedroom and began to prepare for the cold walk to the bridge. She had to do this, but it was the carrying out that she was not prepared for.

"Max I'm going out; I'm going for a walk to clear my head."

Amy was sure that her house was now rigged so she was not allowing herself to give away any details to the monitors. She was not allowing them to steal this from her. She had to have this chat with Emma. It was the only way that their relationship would survive. They had to get over the fence, even if just one of them went, someone was going over that fence.

Amy felt like she was doing the last walk of her life. She felt like she was the only person in the world. She felt truly alone. She passed a few people who lived on her block. She smiled to them politely, but they had no idea the impact of this walk on her life. Amy shuffled along the dark path kicking the gravel as she walked. She would do anything to be doing something else right not, but this had to happen today, now. The walk felt like the longest Amy had ever walked.

It was on the other side of the town, but it was not that far. Amy had been unable to drive the distance, as she normally would, because of the monitors. She did not want them seeing her car missing and knowing that she was not at the house. This was something that she would have to get through without the monitors being able to tell where she was. She could not have the monitors seeing her out at this time of the day, they would ask questions, questions she did not have the answers to.

As Amy was approaching the bridge, she suddenly had a feeling. She was panicking that Emma did not come. What if Emma had completely given up? What if she didn't want to do this and Amy had just turned this into something? Amy wanted to run away. This was the only way that would allow them to live their lives. It was the only way that they could be together, properly. There was no other option. They would have to run away; it was run away or be hanged.

Amy sat on the bench that was situated at the side of the bridge. She hadn't specified the exact place, but she had faith that Emma would know that she meant here. This was the spot that they loved when they were in monitor school. They would come and sit there to watch the river, way before they realised there was anything special with their relationship.

This was the place where it all began, and it was going to be the place where it all ended. For better or worse, they would end this together. It was the only way. Within that moment, Amy realised she had made her decision she knew what she had to do. They were both leaving this place, together, like always.

As Amy was sat thinking she could see a figure approaching her in the distance. This was it. This was the moment that she was going to be the one who had all the answers. She was going to have to be the one, the one who was able to take away all the stress of this situation. The one who was going to make the whole situation easy and the one who was going to rescue it all and make it all better.

"Hey, I figured you meant here. It would make sense I suppose."

Emma grabbed Amy's hand. There was nowhere for her to run. They were in this together, there was no way out for them. They had to be all in or not bother. Amy was glad to see that Emma was with her, she just had to think how to explain the plan to her without showing her panic, or the many holes that were within the plan.

She had this plan all worked out in her head, but Emma was more practical than she was. She would be able to see the holes in this plan; she would be able to see how the plan wouldn't work. This was what was worrying Amy. Would Emma understand the reasons for their running. Would she know why they had to leave. She was hoping that Emma would understand and would see that even though this was not the most reliable plan it was there only plan.

"So, the plan is very much the same as it always has been, however, this plan has to happen soon. Max is still okay to go ahead and he is being amazing with it all. He is very much just wanting a date and then he can put things in place. We will need time to say bye to all the people that we are leaving behind and make sure that things are put in place for when we leave."

"So, all I need to know is whether you are still up for it? Do you want to throw everything away for a wish and a prayer? I know this is not the perfect plan and it means that we are giving up a lot just for this, but I want to be with you, and this is the only way that can do it. Are you in?"

The pause after Amy had finished her speech felt like a lifetime. Amy could see Emma weighing up all of her options. She could see her brain going through the options, all the different answers that there were to that question. Amy was terrified, there was just too much that could go wrong. She suddenly began doubting everything that she had said. The plan was ridiculous, they could not pull it off. How could she have thought that they would be able to escape this hell. No one had been able to escape this place; they were stuck there, forever.

Emma took a deep breathe before answering.

"I know what you are saying, and I know why you are wanting to do this. I completely agree with you we cannot carry on with what we are doing so we do have to think of something, but this is a lot. I don't know if I can do this. I don't know if I will be able to give everything up. This plan means that we will not be able to see our families or our friends ever again. I love you so much, you know I do, but this is a lot. Let me think it over, because this is insane."

Emma knew that she had not said what Amy wanted her to say. She knew that she had let her down. How would she be able to look in her eye after crushing her dreams. She had ruined everything, she had thrown Amy's plan into the dirt and ignored all of her suggestions. Emma wasn't sure what Amy's next move was going to be. She didn't even know if they were still together at this point. She may have ruined everything in that move. She may have completely ruined everything that they had been building. This was it.

Amy was stuck, she couldn't move. She couldn't speak. Emma had thrown her plan out and told her that it would not work, and she was not willing to try. Amy was ready to give up everything for this girl, but she felt like that was not the case for Emma. She did not want to go on living in this place. She had freedom dangled in front of her and she had a plan, it was possible. This was something that could actually happen and now Emma was saying that she did not think it was possible.

Both girls stood looking at each other. Neither of them knew what to say next. How did they carry on after this? They both had different ideas about what they wanted out of life. Was there a way forward after this? How could they carry on, Amy was willing to try anything to live together with the love of her life. But was Emma?

"Em, I need you to do this. Every person gets that one question that they are allowed to ask the person they love. That one question that no matter what the question is the answer has to be yes. This is the question that I am asking you. Please will you do this for me?"

Amy knew that she had crossed a line, she had asked the question. The question that any person was allowed to ask, but it always changes everything. She was nervous. This was the moment where it could all change. She had put the pressure on, this was the moment where Emma could crack. This was the moment where their whole relationship could come crashing down.

Emma knew that she had no choice at this point. This was the moment where she just had to say yes. If she loved Amy, then the answer had to be yes. She did not have a choice. She thought it through slowly, there was no choice she knew what she had to say. She loved this girl and that decided it. She loved her, so the answer had to be yes.

"Amy, you know the answer to that question. You don't have to dress it up like that. I love you, I always will and if you are asking me to do this and you really want to go for it then of course I will go with you. You shouldn't feel like you are alone in this, I back you 100%. When are you planning to carry out this plan?"

"So, its decided, we are doing this. I will let Max know. I will message you with a time and date when I have finalised the details with him. He will be able to put things into action at work and make sure everything is place for when we carry it out. I wouldn't pack too much."

"I have money saved up ready so we will sort ourselves when we get over the fence. It is the only way that we can ensure that we get over the fence safely. I will message you when I have more information and a time. I love you, you know, and I don't think I could ever love anyone but you. I'll see you later, get yourself packed."

Emma knew that she had the decision made for her, she could not say anything else. She had to do this. She wanted to do this; she was just scared.

Both girls stood and looked at each other. Next time they see each other, they would be running away from this place.

Amy grabbed Emma by the waist and pulled her closer. Before either girl knew what was happening, they were locked in a tight embrace.

Chapter 15

The morning after the night before was a strange one for Amy and Max. They had been up most of the night after Amy had come back from her meeting with Emma and had informed Max that the plan was in action. They merely had to pick a date that would work, in regard to who would be on duty at the fence. Max knew of a perfect spot where he would only have to disable one camera to allow the plan to go ahead, which was more believable.

Cameras break quite often so one going out would not cause suspicion. Max had changed the timetable as to who was working to ensure that he was working that night, he could not risk having someone else on the fence at the time of the escape. He was aware that he would probably get hanged for this, but it was something that he had to do.

Amy clicked on the kettle and started to make the coffee. Saturday mornings were always good as both Amy and Max were off work and were able to spend some time together. Although they were not in the relationship that Baskerville had intended, they did have something special. Something that was not easy to explain, but something that was nice to come home to.

Amy switched on the TV to watch the address as she always did every Saturday. There was never a lot on there as people were too afraid to commit any crimes, but there was always an address to the nation on a Saturday morning and it was this that Amy wanted to watch.

All residents were required by law to watch the address. It was the only way to keep the residents up to date with the running of Baskerville, and to ensure that they were aware of any rule change or event that was happening within the town. If your tv was not on in time for the address, then it would come on automatically. There was no excuse for not watching.

"Max, hurry up it is about to start, you don't want to miss it again!"

Max was always late to the address. It had become a weekly occurrence. Amy would have to retell what had been said on it every week. She did not have the energy to do the same today, he would have to watch himself. Amy was not even sure if she had the energy to watch it herself, her brain was spinning with too many things to be worried about what was happening in this god forsaken town.

Amy felt sick, for some reason she had this horrible feeling in the pit of her stomach that this address was not going to be good for her. She had that gut instinct that something was wrong. It was the kind of feeling that you should not ignore.

"Give me a minute, have you got the coffee on? You know I can't face it without my coffee."

Amy poured out the coffee and put the two mugs on the table, she was eager for this to be over. This sick ritual that the town had everyone follow. She could not wait to be over the fence and be able to do what she wanted with her Saturday mornings. In America, people get the whole weekend off and they were allowed to do what they like.

This was something that Amy was eager to take part in, it was something that she was looking forward to. She would be able to do what she wanted with the woman she loved by her side. She could not wait for all this to be a reality and with the plan becoming more and more real. It was looking like she would be able to do this sooner rather than later.

Max sat next her and grabbed his mug, just as the title screen appeared. It was the same as always, bright red with the Baskerville logo blazoned in the middle. This was the moment where Amy's dad would be shouting at the screen 'Hail Baskerville!'.

She never knew why he loved his town so much, but he did, he was the model citizen and what Baskerville wanted all of their residents to be like. That was probably the reason for all his awards. It was not for his work but for his life choices. If he could only imagine what his daughter was about to do, he would probably hang Amy himself.

As the camera panned around the newsroom and zoomed in on the news reader. Amy and Max went quiet.

"Hello and welcome to the Baskerville weekly address, there is a lot to get through today so I will be quick and not take up too much of your Saturday morning."

"There is a new rule coming in as of this afternoon, that if you are to have visitors within your home then they are to register within your household for however long they plan to be within your home. This is to ensure that we know where everyone is, should there be an emergency. You can do this using the location app that should be downloading on your phone as we speak."

"You need to register the household that you are visiting as well as the name of the person that you are visiting. If you are expecting visitors, then you should also log it, using the name and number of the visitor as well as the reason for their visit."

Amy knew this must be a repercussion of the unexpected visit from Emma that they had had the other day. This had to be the reason for this. This was just another way that the town had complete control of the citizen's life. It was the only way that they could keep the town on the straight and narrow. Just monitor everything that was happening.

Amy picked up her phone and sure enough there was an app downloading onto her phone, called location. It was creepy how they could just gain access to the whole town's phones and put whatever they liked on there. It confirmed in Amy's mind that she should not use her phone for anything related to what was happening.

She would use it enough to avoid suspicion, but she would not be using it for her personal life. She would not give the monitors an excuse to take her. This would be something that she would have to do the old-fashioned way, in small areas where the surveillance was not ideal.

"There is also a message just coming through now, that we will be treated to a double hanging this afternoon. As you all know hangings are mandatory attendance, so for those who should be in work, you do not need to attend work. Everywhere will be closed for the rest of the day to allow time for the hanging. Please attend the stocks at 2pm and we will start at 2.30pm."

Amy's heart stopped, why was there to be a hanging, who was being hanged. It was customary for the person that was being hanged to be held in custody before their time, but what if it was her and Emma, and they had just not sent the monitors out yet. The idea of a double hanging was something that was rarely seen. A double hanging happened if there had been two people who had broken the law together.

Two people who had been in it together. That was the only reason for a double hanging. This had to be some kind of cruel joke, was it to be her and Emma. She could not think of any other residents who would be in for a double hanging. She did not know what to do, she had gone cold all of a sudden, like all the blood within her body had been drained. She did not know what to do. She was merely awaiting the knock on the door that would mean that her fate had been sealed.

"I wouldn't worry about it, Amy, it isn't going to be you, you would have been held in custody if it was going to be you. They cannot just spring these things on you, plus you have to be questioned before the hanging. You know that. They would never get it done in time for this afternoon. You are fine don't sweat it."

Amy couldn't believe how Max could be so calm. This was it. Her dreams had finally come to an end. Any minute now there would be a knock on that door. Amy could feel her anger at Max grow. How could he be so calm. This was not a game. This was her life.

"Max, I know your trying to be calm for me, and I know it comes from a good place, but will you shut the fuck up! This could be us, and I could be being hanged this afternoon. Yes, they need to question people before the hanging, but what you have forgotten about is that I have already been questioned! They wouldn't need to question me again. They would simply come to the door grab me and then take me to the stocks. It has happened before, and it will happen again. This is it. I'm dead."

Just as Amy had finished her speech, there was a knock at the door.

"Amy, it's the monitors. Open this door!"

Chapter 16

"Amy, we know you're in there. You have five seconds to open the door before we bash it down and that incurs a fine. Open this door now!"

Amy knew that it was the monitors, she would have to let them in. She had already decided that there was no point in pretending that she was not guilty as it was clear that the monitors already knew about her crimes and they had come to collect her. Amy knew in the pit of her stomach that those two hangings were for her and Emma. Having the monitors here only confirmed this in her head.

"Max what do I do? I don't know if I can let them in. They are after me. I am done. This is going to be the last time you see me, till I am hanging from that rope. I don't know what to do here. There is no training for this, there is no way to be prepared for this."

Max was like he always was. He stood there weighing up the situation so calmly. He was not fazed by anything. Amy had always admired that of him. He was always prepared to deal with whatever the world threw at him. This was something that Amy always loved in him and something that she needed within this very moment.

"Amy, I think there is only one thing that we can do at this moment, we have to open the door. If we do not and they break it down, then we're fucked. Just open the door and see what they want. It may be something of nothing and they just want to speak to you. You never know."

Amy knew that Max was right, she knew that she had to open the door and let these people in. She had to see what these people wanted and why they wanted to speak to her. Max could be right. They might just want to speak her; she did used to work with them after all.

Amy walked over to the door, she had to let them in either way, but she had never been so afraid. This moment was worse than when she had been captured and was in the torture room. This really was her walking to her death. She could see her future as she walked to the door, she was going to be on those gallows any moment and she knew it.

She lifted the latch and opened the door, this was it. This was the end of her life.

There were four monitors at the door, all stood there in their raid gear. They had come for Amy and she knew it, she just had to stay calm.

"Amy, we need you to come in. We are asking you to come into the office just for the hangings. This is not us allowing you back into your job, as you know you have had your licence taken off you, but we need your insights into this case ready for the hangings in a few hours."

Amy was taken back; she did not know what to do. She was not going to die, but she was going to help someone else to. Who were these two people that were being hanged if it was not her and Emma? How was she going to help to send these people to her death when she knows that she should be going to the same fate.

"Okay, I will come with you. Just let me get some things and I will be with you. I presume we will be there for the whole day?"

A strange calm had come over Amy. She knew that she was safe for today, but it was just today. She knew that this was her moment to show the monitors that she was willing to work with them and live within Baskerville's rules. This was her moment to show them all that she was willing to work with them.

If she could do this and get the monitors off her back, she would be able to carry on with her plan and get her and Emma out of this stupid country. Once they were over the fence, all their problems would be over. This was just another step towards her being free with the woman that she loved.

Amy walked with the monitors and got into the car that they had outside her house. They had not come in the marked car which Amy was grateful for. She did not need any more action for the neighbours to see at this point in the plan. They had to think that everything was normal for when she made the great escape. She did not need the neighbours knowing something was going on before she left otherwise when the monitors came to look for them and they interviewed them all individually.

Amy sat in the back as if she was the criminal. This only made her more nervous and her brain started to tick. What if this was all a trick? What if they were simply warming her up to make her think that she was innocent. This could all just be a ploy to get her into the gallows. She may be the one that was being hanged after all.

She was suddenly filled with dread. What if she was going to be the person that was on those gallows later on today. What if she was going to die? What if this was it? Would she be able to deal with standing there, looking onto the crowd, while her and the love of her life prepared to be murdered? Amy did not think that she would be able to deal with watching Emma go through that. She would only have to hope that she died first.

"Okay Amy, so as you know there have been reports of homosexual behaviour in Baskerville. This is something that we want to stamp out. This is not something that we can have here. There is a couple in the lower end of town, who have been together illegally. This is something we need to make an example of so that we can get rid of any other offenders within the area."

"This is where we need your help. You're the person who has the most intelligence when it comes to this. You were on the case when it first began and have the most understanding of this topic. We need your help with the questioning and then we will be taking them to the gallows."

Amy did not know where to look during this conversation. She was the best person for the job, there was no doubt, but it was for all the wrong reasons. She would be able to tell if they were guilty because she was there herself. She would know that if they were guilty or not because she would be able to see it in their eyes.

It would have nothing to do with her interrogation abilities it would all be because she knew how that person was feeling. She knew what was at stake and she knew exactly how the person was feeling. Amy felt sick. She did not know if she would be able to do this. How was she going to decide someone's fate when it should be her on the gallows? She was going to accuse someone of committing the crime that she was committing herself.

Amy walked into the interrogation room. She could not understand why she was even being asked to do this interview, they had already been charged and the hanging was all set up. The general public of Baskerville would be crowded round the gallows in a few hours and they would want to see a hanging.

Once it had been announced that was the end of it, there were no turn backs. These people were certainly being hanged, no matter what Amy was able to find out about them. There was one thing for certain when it came to Baskerville hangings. The person who was being murdered was always guilty.

As she entered the room, she saw her interviewee sitting within the chair. It was the chair that Amy had found herself sitting in not long ago. It was the same chair where she had denied her love for the woman of her dreams and it was the chair where she was close to wishing her whole relationship away. Amy had to put all this behind her, she had to focus on the job at hand. She had to find out as much information about this person as possible, before they go onto the gallows.

"Hello, I am Amy, and I will be interviewing you today. You should know that everything said within this interview will be recorded and saved on the Baskerville database for referral at any time. You do understand the severity of the interview, and what awaits should you be found guilty?"

"Yes."

A muffled voice replied. Amy thought she recognised the voice, and there was something niggling within her that told her that she knew the person that was underneath the pillowcase. She knew that she would have to get the person to take off their covering, but that was against the policy. It was common practice for the interviewee to keep their covering on throughout the interview to add to the pressure that they were under. This would mean that they would be more likely to give up information as they do not know who they were talking to or the torture that could be inflicted on them as they cannot see the torture chamber.

Amy knew the voice and it was bugging her who it could be. She knew that it must be someone that she had met within Baskerville otherwise she would not recognise the voice, but would it make it worse if she knew who she was condemning to the stocks. She knew that was where this person was going. There was no doubt in Amy's mind. The stocks had been booked and there had been an announcement.

The hanging was happening whether Amy gained the information or not. This fact soothed Amy as she knew that there was nothing that she could do. She could simply use this opportunity to her advantage and show the monitors that she was willing to work with them as this would hopefully show them that she had nothing to hide. She was still on probation, so she had to be careful with what she did. This was her chance to show them that it had all been a mistake and she was still willing to put her life on the line for the country.

"As you are aware there have been some reports of homosexual behaviour within Baskerville and this is something that will not be tolerated. Could you confirm for me who you have been assigned as a partner and whether you are living together like partners? I know these questions may seem strange, but they are just the questions that I need to ask in order to file this case."

The man under the covering did not say anything for a very long time. He sat there in silence as though waiting for another prompt from Amy. Amy knew this well and because of her training she knew not to crack. The silence was as uncomfortable for the person being questioned as it was for her, but it was the interviewee's time to talk and they knew that.

Amy would just have to sit there and wait for him to break the silence. This was something that she had been taught at the very beginning of monitor school. Do not break the silence unless it was necessary. It adds an uncomfortable air to the conversation and shows the interviewee who was in charge.

The man sat in silence for a little while longer before he spoke. He conjured up all of his might and whispered something that would haunt Amy for the rest of her life.

"You hypocrite."

Chapter 17

People were already beginning to gather around the stocks, and some were even excited about the idea of having a hanging. This was something that did not happen all that often in Baskerville, so some people were excited about the prospect. Everything had shut early so that everyone would be able to come out to watch. The main aim of the hangings was fear. If the government could put fear in the heads of the community, they would be less likely to break the rules. Because of the lack of hangings, it would seem that the theory was working.

Amy and Max went down to the stocks together. It was common practice for couples to meet and then go down together. Both of them waited on the outskirts for Emma and Kyle. They had decided that this was something that would be better dealt with as a team rather than trying to go through the whole thing individually.

All four of them wandered down into the courtyard. It was not something that any of them were looking forward to. This was something that had to be done. You had to view these things it was policy, but it was not something that Amy wanted to do, and it was not something that she wanted Emma to see. She was too fragile for this. How could the government think this was a good idea?

The trumpet sounded which signalled that everyone should be quiet so that the hangings could begin. The whole crowd fell silent. Some out of fear and some out of excitement. Many people had never been to a hanging before so they were eager to see how it would happen. Curiosity was the main thing drawing them in. There was no one in the community who would wish this on anyone, but it was something that people wanted to see.

"Do you think they will show their faces, or will they have the bags over their heads the whole time?"

Emma was curious but Amy was trying not to think about it.

"Why don't we just wait and see what happens. I am going to try and not look, so just let me know when it has finished!"

Amy did not want to look. It was not for the reasoning that many others were doing the same. Amy did not want to look as this could be her future. This could easily have been her and Emma stood up there. There was a moment when she thought it was going to be her. She had to get out of this crazy town!

After the trumpets, the two men appeared on the stage. They still had the bag over their heads as Amy had predicted but she had a feeling they would not be on there for long. The government would want people to see their faces and to know who was being hanged.

This would happen after they had read out their crimes. the executioner was dressed head to toe in black including a black mask. He looked like something out of a horror film. He stepped forward and pulled a roll of paper out of his hand and began to read.

As he read, Emma slyly grabbed Amy's hand that was resting on her thigh. Amy panicked at first and wanted to pull away. This was far too public of a space to be doing things like this, but she decided against it. In the chaos, no one would be looking at two neighbours who were in the middle of the crowd. Amy gave Emma's hand a squeeze to show her that she was there, and the two girls proceeded to watch the drama unfold.

"We are gathered here today to witness the sentencing and hanging of these two civilians before us. They have been tried and charged with the charge of homosexual behaviour and ignoring the Baskerville code of conduct. This is, of course, punishable by death by hanging. This death shall be carried out within the hour under the surveillance of the whole town. Does anyone object to the charges brought forward?"

This was the moment where someone could do something for these two men. The moment when if someone spoke up it would be taken to a retrial and the evidence would be examined again. This was providing you had a valid reason. No one spoke though. No one ever spoke. It was common within Baskerville that no one would say anything at this moment. There was something inside Amy that was niggling her, but she knew that she could not say anything.

She was already haunted by what the man had said when she had interviewed him. Maybe it was better if these people were hanged. Even as Amy thought it, she knew it was a disgusting thought. How did she end up like this? This town had turned her into the most horrible person. How anyone could love her was beyond her understanding. But she had Emma's hand in her own as reassurance that someone did love her and she had to fight for this woman, no matter what happened.

"If no one has any objections, then the hanging will begin. Please refrain from shouting or throwing things at the charged until the boxes have been removed."

The executioner walked towards the two men and moved them onto the boxes. This was the moment where it all became real for Amy. They really were going to hang these two men. They were going to murder them for doing absolutely nothing wrong. They were being killed for loving someone. This was just not right under any law.

"Em, I don't know if I can watch this. I haven't seen one before in my lifetime and the idea of them being killed for something that I myself am guilty of. I don't think I can do this. I feel like I am going to puke."

"Babe, we just have to stand here and look like part of the crowd. It is the only way that we can get through this. If they think that we are part of the community, then they will be more likely to remove our parole. I can't help feeling like this is a test for us more than anything to see how we will react. We have to act like this does not affect us. We have to pretend that this is just a normal day and we agree with what is happening here."

The executioner walked to the centre of the stage so that everyone could see him. He kept his mask on though, to hide his identity. It was not the best job that you could have been assigned in Baskerville, but their identity was always kept a secret. It was a risky job and if someone found out who the executioner was it could cause chaos for the man who had this job. People would storm the streets to gain revenge on the person who had been hanged and this was not something that Baskerville wanted to encourage.

The masked man was also another way of scaring the community. The idea that the executioner could be hiding within the ranks and no one having any idea who the person was, was more likely to keep people in line. Baskerville had thought of everything when it came to designing this town and the laws that must be obeyed.

When the executioner finally spoke, he gave the speech that was given at the beginning of every hanging. They always explained why the person was being hanged. This was another way of in sighting fear into the community as it showed them what little had to be done to seal your fate in the stocks.

"These are the men that have been breaking the law. These are the men that have been practicing homosexual behaviour in our sacred town. This is why today, with all of you as our witnesses, the town of Baskerville will get rid of these vermin."

Referring to them as vermin seemed a bit strong in Amy's opinion but she knew that she had to blend in with the crown, so she did not let it affect her. She simply squeezed Emma's hand that little bit tighter.

The crowd were growing restless and were eager to see the hanging. It was clear that although it should be something that was wrong the community was eager for one. It was also clear to Amy that the majority of the community seemed to agree that these people should be punished for their behaviour. This scared Amy. How could these people be condoning this kind of behaviour? How could they think that someone should die just because of the person that they loved was not the within the norms.

The executioner came towards the two men and removed their face coverings. The crowd gave out a cheer as their identities were finally revealed. As the boxes were kicked out from under them the crowd exploded. There were people cheering so loud as if they were at a football game. Some people were shouting names at the men and telling them how they were vermin. But it was as the men writhed against the ropes that Amy realised who the man was and why she had recognised his voice earlier that day.

This would explain how he had known that Amy was breaking the law and it would explain how Amy had recognised the voice. This was man who was working alongside Amy when the investigation first began. He knew everything. It was weird to think that the investigation that was launched into this activity included two people within the town who were gay. It was this that caught Amy by surprise. Why had he not said anything? He clearly knew about her and Emma as he had as good as told her that within the interview. There was another question on Amy's mind that she could not ignore. If they knew about them, chances were, they knew about her and Emma too.

Emma squeezed Amy's hand; Amy knew that she was scared. She could tell by the way she was gripping her hand. It was like someone gripping onto their last chance. Amy had to do something. She could not have the girl of her dreams worrying about her life like this. She had to put the plan in action.

92

Just as the scenes did not seem like they could get much worse, the two men stopped writhing. The crowd went quiet. This was it. This was the end. The executioner stood to the front of stage again and addressed the crowd.

"Once again, the Baskerville monitors have achieved their goal and have rid the town of the rule breakers. You need to know that we take rule breaking more seriously than ever and will be cracking down on those who may have got away with it in the past. This is a memorable moment in the town, and it was all thanks to the best monitor of our generation that this could happen. Boris Cleave has worked within the community since he graduated monitor school and he has never drifted from the community once. He will be coming to make a speech very shortly. Thank you for your continued support as we rid the community of vermin like this."

Now Amy knew that she was doomed. Her dad was on the case. He must have been her replacement on the case. This was not a good thing for Amy and Emma. Boris really was the best monitor that had ever been. He probably already knew about Amy and Emma and was simply keeping quiet. Although Amy was not convinced that he would choose her if he was asked to choose between her and his job. It was just a simple fact that her dad's life had always been his job. This could not get any worse for Amy and Emma.

Not only did they have a very good monitor on the case. They had a monitor that had a personal connection with both the girls. They had both stayed at Amy's house at the end of monitor school. Amy could just imagine her dad putting together the pieces as the monitors discovered the evidence to have them both hanged. He would be in a position to testify against them but whether he would or not still remained to be seen.

Once the bodies had been removed from the stage Boris Cleave made an appearance. He was in his full uniform and was adjusting the microphone. This told Amy this was a speech that he had been preparing for a while. He always adjusted his microphone when it was going to be an important speech. It was one of his little ticks. This worried her more, what was he going to say that was going to be so important?

"Thank you again for showing your support for Baskerville and the community that it envelopes. This hanging was another way for us to provide you with the peace of mind that we will punish the rule breakers. These rule breakers in particular were of a certain calibre. The idea of homosexual activity within Baskerville is something that we cannot tolerate. It is not natural."

"If it was what our forefathers wanted, we would all be sectioned off into same sex couples and that is just not what happens here. This behaviour is something that needs to be stamped out as it is not what we want for the community. It is a disgusting act of defiance and it is not something that we condone. This is a warning to anyone who is taking part in this repulsive act that we are cracking down. We have been made aware of an increase in these freaks and we are starting, from today, to exterminate them. That is all, thank you."

Amy was frozen. These words had not come from someone who she did not know. This had come from someone who had seen her grow up and was one of the few people within this mental world that Amy thought she could trust. Amy knew from that warning that it was likely that he already knew about her and Emma. It was just a matter of time before they were arrested. Judging by the speech, Boris was not going to let anyone get away with it, even his daughter. This made it even more real for Amy. She had to do something otherwise her and Emma were going to be on the stocks just like the men earlier.

Chapter 18

"We're just going to have to file her visit. I cannot see how this is such a problem. If we file it, we are making it clear that we have nothing to hide and the monitors won't suspect anything."

Amy could not understand why Max would not get on board with this idea. All that was happening was that Emma was going to come round for the evening for a visit. It wasn't like they were breaking any rules. People were allowed to come into your house and visit each other. This wasn't something that shouldn't be done. Amy just wanted to make sure she did it through the proper channels so that there was no room for error when it came to them seeing each other. Amy did not want the monitors to storm her house again, so she was aware that if she was going to see Emma, she had to do it in the official way so that no one asked any questions.

"I just don't know if you should be admitting that you are meeting up with Emma to the monitors. You are giving them a free pass to arrest you, you are practically admitting to the monitors that you are breaking the law. I just want you to be careful that is all. You know I care about you and I want what is best for you and I just don't think making it public with the monitors is the best way forward."

Amy knew Max was right and she knew that he had her best interests at heart, but he was so frustrating when he had decided something about her life. He did have the element of control sometimes and it was then that Amy saw her father within him.

Amy got out her phone and started to file the visit. She had already told Emma that she should do the same at her end and file her visit to Amy's house. This was something that had to be done officially so that no one could ask any questions. Filing for a visit was something that was very easy to do, but it was something that the monitors had to approve before it happened. This was what worried Amy. If they did not approve of the visit, then the monitors would simply storm the house and arrest them, but this was a chance that Amy had to take. If she did not file it and they were found out, it would look even worse than if they didn't.

"We have to have this chat Max. It is the only way that the plan can get into action and we can get out of this. We have to get out. They are starting to hang people for the exact crime that we are committing. We do not have a choice; we have to go."

Amy was sticking to her guns. This meeting had to take place, and she wanted to see the woman that she loved. It had been too long.

The door rang with the knock that could only be from the one person that Amy wanted to see. Amy ran to the door; she could barely contain her excitement. She was about to see the woman of her dreams behind closed doors for the first time since the monitors had stormed her house. Emma had been scared because of the arrests and had not wanted to get involved with Amy too much to get the monitors off the scent.

But this was something that had to happen as Max had decided that he had the plan in action and they just had to decide when exactly it was going to happen. This was a discussion that they had to have together and something that they had to decide together. It was not a decision that could be taken lightly.

Emma walked in through the door and quickly shut it behind her. It was at this moment that Amy jumped on her. Both girls were wrapped in a tight embrace while Max stood in the background observing. It was moments like this that he knew that he was doing the right thing. He had to help these women to get out of this hell hole. There was no doubt in his mind that this was the right thing to do.

Emma pulled Amy towards her and kissed her harder than she had ever kissed her before. The idea that the plan could be coming together very soon seemed to have ignited a flame inside her that someday they could be living like a normal couple.

For both girls, time stood still. For once, neither one of them was worried about the outside world. They did not give it a second thought. They were fully involved in the kiss. Nothing could have broken this till they decided.

The kiss seemed to last a lifetime and both girls were so engrossed by it that it seemed that it would never end. Emma's hands started to drift from Amy's head and shoulders down her body as Amy did the same. Both girls had forgotten that they had an audience because of the intensity of the kiss. The kiss began to get deeper and both girls were so engrossed by each other that they had little time for the outside world. Before long, Amy was preparing to undress Emma when Max felt like he should remind them that he was in the room.

It was Max's subtle cough that broke up the girls. He didn't want to get in between them but he didn't know where this was about to go and he felt like he should do something before it escalated.

"Sorry Max got a little carried away there. I just haven't seen her for so long."

Amy was suddenly embarrassed by what had just happened. She knew that Max did not mind but she did not like the idea of someone being there while her and Emma were having their special moment.

"You can be together soon, but we need to sort out this plan to get your out of here so that it becomes a permanent thing rather than stolen moments. Sit down, I'll put the kettle on."

Amy was still shocked at how kind and amazing this man was. If only she could have made it work with him, it would have been a lovely relationship. Amy was a little sad that it did not work out with her and Max as she believed that she could have been happy with him and lived a nice life. It was too late for that though; she had met the person that she wanted to spend the rest of her life with. It was just not quite so accepted within Baskerville which was why the plan had to happen.

"Do you think we can actually do this, just run away? I have never known anyone be able to do it before. What if we are caught? We will be hanged for sure and that will be the end of it. I'm scared. I don't know if I can do this."

Emma was scared and Amy knew it. It was a big thing that they were doing. They were going to run away, out of the craziness of this town and enjoy life in America. This was something that both girls had only dreamed of up until now. But now, with Max's help, they were going to be able to get out of the town and live their lives free from the constraints of Baskerville.

When max came back into the room, both girls were snuggled up together on the sofa. They both looked so peaceful. It was times like this that Max knew that he had to do this. He was risking his life to be able to provide this escape route for the girls, but in his heart, he knew he had to do, no matter what was on the line.

He set the coffee's down on the table and pulled out his drawings. He had been working hard on the plan and he wanted to be thorough, which was why he had the drawings. He had been planning this for months. He laid out the drawings and began to explain his plan. As he was talking it was clear that he was proud of his achievement and that his plan was coming together. You could hear the pride in his voice as he spoke, and he pointed to different parts of the drawing to aid his explanations.

This was something that he had been working on for a long time and he had thought about all the loopholes that there might be. This was when Amy knew that she had the right person on her side. She had done a good thing telling Max about her relationship and she did truly think it was the best thing that she had done. They could never have thought of this plan themselves and they needed Max's expertise from the guard in order to even get near the fence, never mind go under it.

Emma was engrossed in what Max was saying. The idea that they could be free very soon was something that she had been looking forward to for a very long time. This was going to be the moment when her and Amy could finally be who they wanted to be. Emma had been saving up the little money that she had been earning so that they could find somewhere to live and then she could start doing whatever she wanted to do. She had only ever been trained to be a monitor, but she was eager to try something else. Anything else but live in this crazy town.

"So, this is all in action. This is really going to happen. I can't actually believe it. You have performed a miracle Max. I didn't doubt you for a second. So, when is the big day?"

Max had thought this through very carefully as well. He did not want anyone to be at the fence when he snuck the girls through so he had given some of the guards the night off and said that he would be able to manage his section of the fence. This was not an odd occurrence.

Max would often give his men a night off so that they could spend time with their families, so the others did not find this suspicious. Max had been planning this for a while and had made a habit of letting the guards have the odd day off so that it would not look odd when he did it to get the girls out. He really had thought of everything.

"I have planned for it to go ahead on Wednesday. This gives us enough time for the chaos over the hangings to die down and it means that we can have a quiet town when it happens. This is what we want as we do not want too many people to notice what is happening. The only piece of advice I can give you is to leave your phones at home. I am sure there are tracking devices in them so do not take them with you."

"You can buy another one when you get out and settled, but do not take it with you. Amy I wouldn't even risk taking your burner. You know what they are like it could have a chip hidden inside it either way. Leave everything here. You can take some essentials, but you are going to have to travel light. I cannot get big things through the fence so please don't try and bring everything. Just the essentials. That is all you will need."

Max was very matter of fact in what he was saying, but he was right. This was something that had to be done properly, he could not risk getting caught and the only way to ensure he didn't get caught was to make sure that the girls were able to get out of the town as quick as possible. He was nervous about the whole thing. It was not just his job that he was risking, it was his life. If the monitors found out what he was planning he would be hanged for sure, but this was a risk that he was willing to take in order for the girls to be free to live a life together.

Amy and Emma were quiet for a while. This was it. They were finally going to be free to live their lives the way that they wanted to without having to hide away and fear for their lives. This was what they had wanted from the beginning. Although both girls were eager to get away from Baskerville, the idea of leaving in three days' time was nerve wracking. They would have to prepare to leave and get sorted all within that time and without anyone realising what was happening. This was it; they were finally going to be free.

"I think you two need some time to process what I have just said so I am going to go for a walk and then go to the shops. I'll leave you in peace for a while so you can mull it all over and think about how this is going to work for you two."

Max went to leave the girls alone, he gave Amy a loving wink which told her that he would be gone for as long as it took. He truly was the best man Amy had ever known.

Chapter 19

Max had left the house and the girls had not moved from the sofa. They had been sat talking about what life was going to be like for them and how they would survive in the world. They had been discussing what they would do for a living and how they were going to make their money. Amy had decided that she was going to try and get a job in law as the idea of being able to work for a fair justice system seemed like the best place for Amy to use her skills that she had learnt in monitor school.

Emma had decided she didn't want anything to do with law or telling other people what to do. Her time in the ranks had not been as smooth as Amy's and she wanted a simpler life. She was thinking of retraining when they got out and doing something a little more physical and rewarding.

The girls were led, snuggled together on the sofa looking out the window at the crazy world that they were about to leave behind. They could not believe that were about to escape this crazy world. This was the dream. This was what they had both been waiting for this whole time. This was the end of the torture.

"I can't believe we are actually going to be able to do this. This is it for us now. This will be real life. We will be able to do this whenever we want and not have to worry about who is going to come through the door. It is going to be amazing. I cannot wait to spend my life with you."

Amy was flattered by what Emma was saying. She could not wait to spend her life with Emma either. They were both starting to think about the future, something neither of them had done for a very long time. They were going to be free.

Amy leaned in and kissed Emma so deeply that Emma could feel the emotion pouring in through it. This was true love, and nothing could ever match it.

The kiss between them began to grow deeper, both girls were enthralled by each other and had suddenly forgotten about the outside. There was only the two of them, wrapped together under the blanket as if it somehow protected them from the outside world. Emma flipped Amy over to enable herself to lie on top of Amy and pin her down. Although Emma was not as bold in life as Amy, she was definitely bolder in the bedroom.

"I could not think of a better way to spend my life than to be with you every minute of every day."

The idea of living like this for the rest of her life only turned Amy on more. The woman that she loved was led on top of her and pinning her to the sofa. She could not move even if she wanted to. Emma was moving down her body now, caressing every inch of her as she went. She managed to gain entry into Amy's brain every time and show her that true pleasure could only be found when they were together.

As Emma went further down, Amy let out a small moan. She could not believe that this was happening again. She had only invited her over to discuss them escaping. This was not part of the plan. Amy suddenly became aware of where she was and the outside world that was on the other side of the front door. The door was staring at her and Amy had visions of it slowly disappearing and displaying this to the outside world. Her mind had gone. She needed to be with Emma, but she could not lie with her like this when the door was staring her down.

"Do you want to take this upstairs? I can't deal with that door, its staring me down."

"We can do whatever you want to babe, we are nearly free, and I think that calls for some sort of celebration."

The girls ran up the stairs hand in hand. They were like two love struck teenagers whose parents had left for the weekend. This was one of the small moments that they got together in this crazy town and although this was the end of many things, the girls saw it as the beginning of their lives.

Once in the bedroom, Amy threw Emma onto the bed. She had decided that she was going to take charge of this and be more assertive. She had been wanting to do it for a while, but Emma was so authoritative in these situations, which Amy found incredibly sexy. But she had decided that she was going to take the wheel and show Emma what she could do.

Emma obliged to Amy taking charge and let her jump on top of her. This was not a position that Amy was used to, but it was something that she was enjoying trying out. Amy had never taken charge like this and Emma presumed she was charged from the news that they were going to be free.

The girls began kissing again as Amy started to undress Emma. She wanted to feel her, all of her and just being skin on skin with this incredible woman was enough for Amy. This woman was all she needed in life. As long as she had her, she had everything she needed.

Amy began to work down Emma's now naked body, having her there in front of her was overwhelming for Amy and it was turning her on no end. Emma began to writhe against Amy's body showing the pleasure that she was experiencing from Amy's touch. Amy carried on working her way down Emma's body kissing her as she went. As she arrived at Emma's point, she discovered that her work had been successful.

Emma was ready for her, as Amy ventured inside, she could feel the tension within Emma and her need for Amy to do more. She moved her fingers in a rhythm and began to pleasure Emma in a way that she had never done before. Emma let out a small squeal that allowed Amy to know that she was doing it right. In order to tease, Amy simply stopped and went back to kissing her, her touch was light, like the wind on a summer's day. This only engaged Emma further and teased her into submission.

Emma could not take Amy being in charge any longer and flipped her over with the strength of a bull. Emma was now in charge. The girls writhed around the bed like two lioness' fighting for their pride. This was not soft and gentle; this was rough and ready and passionate fuelled love making. Emma felt her way down Amy's body with her tongue.

Amy knew what was coming but she was not prepared for the feeling. Emma's tongue greeted her in a way it had never before and as Emma proceeded to pleasure Amy, she began to smile. Amy bucked under the pressure of Emma's tongue which only greater increased the pleasure, Amy let out a scream that could only mean that she was close. Closer than she had ever been before.

When the tension dissipated from Amy's body, she let out the most extraordinary scream. This scream told Emma that she had done her job.

Amy had gone limp, she felt abused. Emma slowly came back up from where she had been lying and grabbed Amy into a warm embrace. Cupping her breasts into her hands.

"You know, we're going to be able to do that all the time soon. How good will that be. You practice those new moves whenever you like."

Emma's voice was still soft and flirty, she talked to Amy as if she was teasing her. Amy could not believe she still had the energy for talking, she was done.

"I don't know if I will be able to do that all the time. I don't think I would have the energy. You zap the energy right out of me, and I don't know how."

Emma was pleased to hear that she had been successful in her mission and led there quietly while Amy fell asleep in her arms. It was when Amy was asleep that Emma was most in love with her. She looked so peaceful; she was not weighed down by the anxiety that life filled her with. She was free to be whatever she wanted to be in her dreams. This was when Emma saw the real Amy and she hoped that this would be the new Amy once they got out of this crazy town.

Chapter 20

There was a lot to do in order to get the plan ready in time for Wednesday. Amy had decided that she would go around to her parents to say her goodbyes. She knew it was something that she would have to do before leaving otherwise her parents would never forgive her. She had to say goodbye. Even if it was not really saying goodbye.

She had rung her mother who had organised for her father to be home for dinner so that Amy could see them both. It was decided that they should have dinner together as a nice change. Within Baskerville, eating at another person's house can be challenging because of the rations, but Amy was going to bring her ration for that night so that her mother could cook with it and create a dinner for three.

Amy was nervous about the dinner; she didn't know what she was going to say to her parents when she went in or why she was having dinner. She didn't know what she was going to say when they asked about Max. She didn't have the answers that they would want, but she had to see them one last time before she left.

As Amy got into her car to go to her parents Max ran out with some flowers.

"Thought your mum might like these, make you look like you made an effort. I know this is a weird one, but make sure you don't say anything too incriminating to your father. You know what he is like. Just be careful is all I'm saying. We don't want the plan to fail at this point when it is going so well."

Even now, Amy was still shocked at the amazingness of this man. He truly did care about Amy and what happened to her, he really was one of the good guys in this crazy town.

"Thanks Max, I didn't think about that. You really are amazing."

Amy gave him a hug and jumped in her car. This was going to be a weird experience for her, but it was something she was just going to have to get through. And like Max had said, she had to be careful with what she said. She could not have her father finding out about her plans, as that would be the end.

Amy turned her car into the large driveway of her parents' house. Boris really did have one of the nicest houses in Baskerville. This was what Amy had been striving for until she met Emma. She had wanted to live on this street and be one of the best monitors, carrying on her dad's legacy. She had no idea that her life would fall into such turmoil just from one girl.

Amy's mum answered the door and was pleased when Amy presented her with the flowers. Amy did not often show affection to her parents and rarely came to visit so it was nice for her to be able to gain something from her daughter, however small.

"Hello darling, how are you doing? I was a little worried when I got your call asking for dinner. You don't often come and see us anymore. You seem to have gone a little under the grid."

"I know Mum, sorry. I had just been busy with work and getting settled in with Max and everything, so it's been a little chaotic at my end. How have you been?"

Amy wasn't sure if her dad would have told her about her losing her job and being on probation, so she did not mention that she was not at work at the moment. She did not want to upset her mother any more than she was about to when she left. She knew that it would hit her the hardest as she was the only person who truly loved her aside from Emma.

As Amy entered the house, she could already smell her mother cooking something. She really was good in the kitchen. Amy had been spoiled as a child as her mother was able to make really good meals out of the rations that were issued by the government. Not everyone had been so lucky. She knew that Max had spent most of his life living off the breakfast gruel that was so popular within Baskerville, purely because his mother did not know what to do with the rations that were provided for them.

As they waited for Boris to return from work Amy helped her mother in the kitchen like she used to do when she was a child and they talked about life in general and how Amy was settling into Baskerville life. Janet did not ask too many questions so that her daughter could talk freely about her life and how she was getting on. Amy was careful with what she told her mother and made it clear to her that her and Max were getting on well and were adjusting to living in their big house. This was not a lie, her and Max were getting along well. But it was not in the way that Janet expected them to be.

"I know that me and your father are a strange case, but I do hope that you will be able to bond with this boy and be able to live a happy life. I am hoping for some grandchildren you know!"

It was this that killed Amy. She was robbing her mother of a normal life; her mother would never see her grandchildren. She would never attend her daughter's wedding and she would definitely not be having family Christmases. All these factors that Amy had not thought of suddenly hit her. All the things that she was robbing her mother of. Amy suddenly realised how selfish she was being living this lifestyle.

She wanted to confess right there, but she knew that she couldn't. It would blow the whole plan. She would have to remain strong and know that what she was doing was for all the right reasons. She wanted to be with Emma and nothing her mother said would make her change her mind.

Just as Amy was losing will power and wanted to spill everything to her mother, her father entered the house. Boris Cleave was the kind of man that took over a room as soon as he entered it. Amy suddenly became very uncomfortable. How was she going to carry on with this charade and not tell them everything that was happening.

Amy was sure that he already had a good idea of what was going on with him being assigned the case and being presented with the evidence. Her and Emma going in for questioning was enough for him to throw her out of house. Amy did not know which way this dinner was going to go. She could only hope, for her mother's sake, that her father did not say too much.

"Hello Janet, my dear, dinner smells nice as ever! Have you had a nice day?"

Amy was reminded of her parents love and how much they did care for each other. It was a warming feeling that two people could find love in this horrid town.

Boris had seen Amy but did not acknowledge her at first. He was thinking through how he was going to approach the situation. He wanted Amy to know that he knew everything, but he did not want his wife to see that something wrong. He decided to acknowledge her and that was it.

"Amy, lovely of you to join us. I thought you would be too busy with your little life to come and see us. You usually are."

That was all Amy needed to know that her father knew everything. The way he had used his tone suggested he knew exactly what, or rather who, was in Amy's little world.

"Now, now, Boris play nice, Amy has come round for dinner and to see us both. Isn't that nice?"

You could have cut the tension within the room with a knife. It was clear that Boris knew that his daughter had disappointed him, but he was putting on a brave face for his wife. Amy would have to get through this dinner as best as she could without giving anything away. This was the last time she was going to see her parents so she could not mess it up.

Overall, the dinner went smoothly. No questions were asked, and all the family got on like they always had done. They talked about mundane things and asked about Amy's life. Boris did not say much, however, and simply ate his food while Amy and Janet talked about life. It was difficult for Amy to understand what her father was going to do. He had made it clear that he knew, but he had obviously not told her mother as she was talking away to Amy like everything was normal.

Amy began to be very wary of her father. She never thought of it until now, but her father may just hand her into the monitors at the end of this meal. She was hoping with every inch of her being that he wouldn't. Even if it was just for her mother's sake. Amy definitely did not trust him, and that was a feeling that Amy was not enjoying. She had always looked up to her father and thought he was the best person in the world, but this was a different feeling.

This was unease. Amy did not know if it was because she had seen him up on the stocks two days earlier or whether it had just suddenly become clear to her that her father would always put the job first before her, but she did not like the idea that the man who could ruin everything for her was, not only sat opposite her at the table, but her father.

Throughout the dinner Boris continued to say nothing. This only made Amy more wary.

"Why are we so tense? This is meant to be a nice night for all of us. It is not often that Amy comes back to see us, so we should be enjoying this night. Boris, dear, have you had another stressful day at work? There must be some reason why you are sitting there like that."

Amy was terrified, her mother had poked the bear. She did not know what her father was going to say but she knew that she wasn't going to like it. This could be it. This could be the moment when her father betrays her. Amy was sure that he knew everything, not only that she was on probation but the reason that she was on probation. He could get whatever information he wanted because of his ranks and it would only take a quick search on the system to explain everything. She did not know what was going to be said, but she knew deep down, that it wasn't going to be good for her.

"It has just been a stressful day Janet, with the hangings on Sunday everyone has started reporting homosexual activity constantly. Half the time it is just two good friends, but there is one report that I need to look into further. One that is quite disturbing."

There were no prizes for guessing which report was disturbing him. He had made eye contact with Amy as he had said it, so Amy knew it was her name that he was thinking of. Amy had to get out of there she needed a minute to breathe.

"Can I just nip to the bathroom. I won't be long."

She knew this did not look good to just run out after her father had said those words, but she could not stand to sit there while her father talked about her with such disgust. Amy only just got to the toilet in time before she saw her dinner again. Her stomach was emptying itself as though that would fix everything. Amy did not often puke so this came as a surprise to her. What her father had said had really shocked her.

How could he say those things and with such disgust? This was her life. It was clear that if the truth did come out then Amy and Emma were screwed. They would both be on that stage by the weekend and Amy knew this. She had to get out of here. The escape was planned for tomorrow so she only needed one more sleep and it would all be over. She would just have to get through this dinner and then she would be fine.

After sorting herself out and lifting her tired body up off the floor, she went back to the dining room where her parents were eagerly awaiting her.

"Are you okay sweetheart? I thought I heard puking in there? You haven't eaten anything funny, have you? Oh, you could be pregnant, how good would that be!"

Another heart-breaking moment. She could personally guarantee that she was not pregnant it was biologically impossible, but her mother was not to know.

"I can assure you she is not pregnant."

The same tone of disgust. Boris did know and he was making it plainer every minute.

When dinner was over, there was an awkwardness where Amy knew she had to leave now and say goodbye to her parents for the last time. This was what Amy had come to do and this was why she had dealt with her father all night, she had to say goodbye.

Amy was gearing herself up to say goodbye to her parents when her father called her aside. She knew this was not going to be a nice conversation, but she had a feeling she was about to learn how much her father knew. This would allow her to gain a fuller picture of what she had to hide from him. She had no doubt that he knew the majority of it, but she wanted to know exactly what he knew. She just didn't want her mother to know about any of it, she didn't think that she would be able to handle it.

"Janet, I need to have a conversation with Amy before she leaves. It is just work stuff so I will take it into the study, so we do not disturb you."

This was good. He was not going to tell her mother. Amy breathed a sigh of relief at the thought of her mother still being blissfully unaware of her crimes against the state. She could not deal with the idea of her mother being disappointed in her.

Boris guided Amy into the study, she did not have a choice. This conversation had to happen no matter what. She wanted it to be a pleasant conversation as this was going to be the last time that she saw her father, so she wanted it to be a nice thing for her to remember.

"Amy, what the fuck are you doing!"

He shouted in a way that scared Amy. He did not often shout, so when he did it caught her off guard. She did not know how to reply. He was right what the fuck was she doing? Her life was spiralling, and she could not stop it. But she had made her decision and she knew what was going to happen she just had to hope that her father did not know.

Amy did not know how to reply. She did not want this to become an argument she wanted this to be a nice conversation, but Amy was slowly realising, that ship had sailed.

"Dad, I know you know the majority of what is going on and honestly in answer to your question I have no idea. My life is spiralling out of control and I don't know how to stop it. I am trying and Max is amazing, and I do love him but not in the way I love her. Dad, I need your help. How can I make this work?"

Amy didn't know what she had done. It had all just come spilling out and she couldn't stop it. She shouldn't have been so open with him, but she couldn't help it. He was her last chance at potentially living here like this. He could do something about this crazy world, and he might be able to change the path of things.

"There is no way you can make it work. You have been identified as a criminal for fuck's sake. What am I supposed to do when my only daughter is breaking the law that I have to police? Do you know how bad that makes me look? And you cannot say that you were even careful, the monitors found you in bed together in your house. There was a report of you two together in a car on the street, Amy, anyone could have seen you there. I cannot believe that you have done this, I cannot believe that you have dragged my name through the dirt. How will I ever gain the respect of Baskerville back after this?"

"There is no getting out of it, you know what I have to do. I have ordered for a hanging to take place at the weekend, I wanted to tell you myself so that you would know before the monitors come and take you away. I am sorry Amy, but I am stuck between a rock and a hard place here, so this is the best thing for everyone. I don't know how I am going to tell your mother that but that is my job. I will deal with her; you do not breathe a word to her. I cannot imagine what is running through your head right now, but you have to understand that I do not have a choice.

"This is the only thing that I can do without bringing great shame on the family. Go back home and prepare. If you want to tell Emma, then tell her but it might be better if she doesn't know that you know that way, she cannot blame you for what is happening. The monitors will pick you up on Thursday, so make sure you are home. It is best for everyone if you go quietly Amy."

"I know this is not the ending that you were wanting, and I know that it must be hard, but you have to understand that I cannot have that behaviour within my town, and it must be put to an end. And I'm afraid in Baskerville there is only one punishment for all crimes. Death. I cannot believe what you have done. You have tarnished this name, and for that you will hang."

Boris was so calm after his speech; it was as if he had just delivered it to another citizen of Baskerville and not his own daughter. Amy could not believe it. He really had filed for her to be hanged. He had chosen the job over her. She always knew it was possible, but she wasn't sure if he would go through with it, but he had and that was that. Amy could barely look at him. He had filed for his own daughter to be hanged purely because she did not follow the stupid rules of one stupid town.

Amy broke, she fell to the floor and stayed there curled up. How could he do this. The one man in the world who she thought would always have her back had personally caused the end of her life. It was not so much the prospect of being hanged that upset Amy, as she would be leaving before the monitors came to get her, but it was the fact that she had been betrayed. She had no words left to say to her father as she did not want to interact with him anymore. He had lost all rights to call her his daughter. That was it. They were over.

Amy ran into her car and rammed it into reverse. She knew it wasn't the car's fault, but it was the only thing she could take her out anger on right now, so she took it. She knew where she was driving, the one place that she should not be going. Especially now when the monitors were after her and would no doubt be watching her. But she had to see the one person in the world who could make this all better.

Boris had told her not to tell Emma but that was because Boris thought that his daughter was being hanged on Saturday. That was just not the case, they were escaping tomorrow, and nothing had confirmed it more in Amy's head than the meeting with her father. There was no other option now. The element of choice had been whittled away. They had to leave tomorrow, before the monitors came to arrest them, and before they were hanged.

Amy rammed her car into Emma's drive. She wasn't being discreet, and she knew it, but she was starting to not care. They were getting out of this hell hole shortly and then it would all just feel like a bad dream. As she approached Emma's door, she suddenly thought that she hadn't logged her visit on the system. She didn't think that she would be that long, so she left it.

Chapter 21

Emma was surprised to see Amy at her door and a little confused. She could not understand why Amy would be at her house. Unless it had gone really badly with her parents, but she had not gained the notification that she was expecting a visit which meant that Amy had not logged it on the system. This worried Emma as this was the exact thing that the monitors would be waiting for so that they could hold them in custody. They could not be put in custody as that would affect their chances of escape. Emma was relying on them getting out tomorrow night as it was their only chance at living a normal life and not having to live a life of shame.

"Babe, what are you doing here. You are going to get us both killed if you do not follow protocol. When you come and visit me, you need to log the visit. You said yourself we need appear as if we are doing nothing wrong."

Emma was beginning to panic. By not complying with the rules, they were both at risk, she could not deal with being in custody again. That had been the hardest night of her life.

"I am sorry, I just needed to tell you something in case there was any doubt in your mind about tomorrow. I have just spoken to my father and he has informed me that he has filed for us both to be hanged this week. He said that we would be picked up on Thursday, so we definitely need to go tomorrow. There is no other option for us. If you do not come with me, you will be hanged so please. If there is any doubt in your mind, you need to deal with that and get over it because we cannot stay here anymore, we have been named."

Emma did not know how to react. Boris has filed for the hangings himself. She did not know what to think about that. She knew he always valued his job, but she did not think that he would put his job before his daughter. This was the proof that Emma needed to know that Baskerville was not the town for them. They either left tomorrow and went to America, or they hanged. There was no other option at this point.

"There is no other option then. We will have to leave tomorrow. I cannot wait to start my life with you."

Amy was relieved. She had a moment where she thought Emma would duck out, but this must have been the final push that she needed to go ahead with the plan. Amy knew now, more than ever that this girl was the love of her life.

"I need to go now before anyone realises, I am here, but I will see you tomorrow when we leave this stupid town. I love you, more than you can even imagine."

Both girls stood face to face looking deeply into each other's eyes. They knew they shouldn't but with the joy of finally getting out looming over their heads they could not help it. They both leaned in simultaneously and kissed. Both girls were locked together, hands travelling around each other's bodies, like ants on an ant hill. Longing for more but knowing that it was impossible. They were stuck there. Both of them knowing they had to let go, but neither of them being able to.

It was only when the door broke down that the two girls fell apart.

"This is the monitors. We have reason to believe there is homosexual activity happening here in this house. Is this true? Please be warned that anything said from here and now could be used against in the trial."

Emma and Amy were frozen in fear. This was it. There life was over.

The deafening scream that came from Emma at this point curdled Amy's insides. She had put this woman in danger and now they were both going to pay. This was it. What her father had been talking about. It was going to happen.

The monitors grabbed Emma first and handcuffed her, she went quietly and didn't say another word. Amy was kicking and screaming as the monitors were bundling her up and pushing her into the car. Amy watched the car containing the woman she loved drive away and leave her. She had never felt more alone.

How could she have done this to her?

Amy continued to scream, but it did not affect the monitors; they were immune to it all. They did not seem bothered in the slightest at what was happening in the back seat of the car. All they seemed to care about was that they had got them.

"The boss is going to be so pleased with us, I knew it when I saw that car. I told you!"

Amy had no doubt in her mind who the boss was. Her father. She was starting to believe that her father had done this to her. He would have known that after hearing what he had to say that she would go round to Emma's. it was him that had ordered the raid. It was him that had caused all this.

The anger inside Amy rose like a serpent, wrapping around her and consuming her. She was no longer upset or worried. She was livid.

Amy was kicking and screaming in the back of the car, while the monitors were taunting her. She could not contain her anger; she was thrashing against the pressure of the handcuffs. She was like a wild animal being captured. There was no going back from here for her. She had to do something drastic. Amy knew that the monitors had already sentenced her to death so nothing she could do was going to make this worse.

She knew that she had to be at home tonight for the plan to take action and she refused to let the plan go just yet. She bottled up all her strength and punched the handcuffs against the window of the car. The glass shattered into pieces and fell like crystals. This was her chance.

The smash had caused the monitors to stop the car and look back to check what the damage had been. All they could see was a smashed window and a broken girl. Amy's arms were pouring with blood, as she sat huddled in the back seat wailing.

She just couldn't do it. Amy could have ran out of that car and tried to save herself, but what was the point in surviving this when the love of her life was still trapped in the car in front? Amy had lost all her fight; she did not have an ounce of will power left within her. She had started well and mustered all her strength to smash that window, but it had all disappeared once the window was smashed.

Amy looked down at her arms that were now bright red with the blood that was pumping out of her veins. She didn't care. She couldn't even feel the pain that she was sure she must be feeling. All her emotions had ran out. She had nothing left to give; she was done.

"We're going to have to put her in the medical room when we get back mate. She's full of blood. I'll put the emergency window on and then we can get her back."

It astonished Amy at how little they seemed to care about the fact that she was, effectively, bleeding to death. They did not bat an eyelid when they saw her wounds. They simply carried on with what they were doing. One of the monitors installed the emergency window and then they began to drive again.

Amy was lifeless. She had had her chance to run and to get away from this, but she had not taken it. Why had she been so weak? She knew deep down why she hadn't run. What would be the point of running when she had nowhere to run to? If she ran out of the car, what would she achieve? She would not be able to live freely and she would not have the woman she loved by her side so there really was no point in her running at this stage. She had to stay to protect Emma. Amy had accepted that they were both going to be hanged, but she was going to make damn sure that the monitors did not do anything to Emma before that day that would make this situation even more miserable.

As the cars pulled up to the monitors headquarters Amy knew that there was nothing else for her to do. This was the end of everything. The end of everything she had been working towards. All her hard work and effort had been for nothing. She would have to live with the consequences. A sad thought entered her head as she thought this.

At least, I won't have to live with it for long.

Chapter 22

The dankness of the cell was starting to seep through Amy's clothes. She was starting to feel the cold as the night drew in. There were no lights in the cell, there was only a small glimmer of light that came from the hallway. Everything in the cell was cold. It was all metal and concrete that leeched the heat from your body like a vampire. The only source of warmth were the damp sheets on the bed. Amy almost felt colder within the sheets than she did on the floor, due to them being damp. She could not imagine that Emma would be coping with these conditions. She hated the cold and she always felt it before Amy did. She was that person who was always cold so she would be freezing.

Amy led on the cot that was meant to be her bed. She was examining her cell in detail in the tiny shred of light that peeked through her cell bars. She could see the walls and ceiling with peeling paint where it had obviously once been decorated, many years ago. The cold, unforgiving concrete floor that she had been led on earlier was discoloured in a way that told Amy that it was hosed down regularly. Why it had to be hosed down was something that Amy did not want to know.

Although there were rarely hangings in Baskerville, the cells were always a busy place while people were being held before questioning. They were usually found innocent after spending days in these conditions. Amy was sure it was another scare tactic that the government used to keep the civilians in line. How had she worked for them? How could she have even gone along with their rules and trained to be one of them for the best part of her life? On the concrete floor were three iron loops. Amy knew what these were for as she had taken the training for using the loops.

There were three loops spaced around two metres apart. These were for tying up the prisoners who were being particularly hard work. It was a way of keeping them under control. Amy could not see when they would be needed.

Amy then took her attention to her arms. She had been bandaged up in the medical room as soon as she had got to the headquarters. Her arms had been pumping with blood, the car had been covered. Amy was impressed that she was still standing, considering the amount of blood she had lost. She had tight bandages all up her arms to stop the bleeding. She had also been given some pain killers. Amy could not understand why they had bothered giving her painkillers when she was so close to being killed. She could not see why they would want her to be killing off pain when they were about to inflict more on her. She knew that they would want to interview her before the hanging. Even if it was just for their own sadistic pleasure.

Emma had been confined to a similar cell as Amy. As Amy had predicted she was very cold. Emma had never been good with cold. She always needed an extra blanket on her at night and she always wanted a hot bottle at night to allow her to sleep while she was warm. She really was terrible with the cold. She too was led in the cot, but she did not have the resolve that Amy had. She was led, crying.

The idea of being hanged was killing her. This was the end of her life. How was she going to have the guts to stand up in front of the whole town with the love of her life while the whole town came out to cheer her death. She did not know if she would be able to face it. She couldn't face it. This was it for her. Emma had not managed to tell her parents before she was arrested. She had planned to speak to her parents that evening. They would be wondering where she was. Emma didn't worry about them too much.

They would understand as soon as the bulletin went out with the names of those being hanged on it. Then they would know why she had not turned up for their dinner. They would know why too. Emma had an inkling that they knew what was happening between her and Amy, but she had shrugged it off and not taken it any further. She had always wanted to tell them but there was never the right time. Emma did not think her parents would mind. In order to care about something like that, they would have to care about Emma first, and that was never going to happen.

Emma's parents were the kind of family that were found a lot within Baskerville. They were two people who had been forced to live together and be a couple when they had nothing in common and had no feelings towards each other. It was not that they did not like each other, it was just that they did not have any feelings towards each other. They lived together in harmony but that was it. Emma sometimes thought they only had her so the neighbours would stop staring. In Baskerville, it was weird to not have children.

For some reason, everyone in the town felt it was their duty to have a child to help Baskerville live on. This was not something that Emma could get behind. She could not think of anything worse than bringing a child into this world, but she could understand why her parents had done, because of the peer pressure of this stupid town!

The cold was creeping into Emma's cell quicker than she could cope with. She was going to freeze to death if it didn't warm up soon. She did not know how it had got to this. All she had done was be with the love of her life. How was this world so cruel? She lay, wrapped in the small blanket that was on the bed and hoped for warmth. All Emma wanted in this moment was for Amy to get into bed with her.

Amy always managed to keep her warm when it was cold, even on the coldest nights in Baskerville. Emma did not understand why it was so cold. It was not the winter and Baskerville rarely got cold in the winter. She wondered if it was there for effect. It would not surprise her. It would be another form of torture that the monitors could use to get what they wanted out of the prisoners. It was cruel. This whole situation was cruel.

That night was the longest night of Emma's life. She did not sleep at all throughout the night and was sat worrying about Amy. It was hard for Emma, undoubtably, but it was even harder for Amy as it was her own father that had reported them and signed the sanction for them to be hanged. Emma was worrying about Amy she did not know how she was coping with all this. Emma knew that she was strong, but there was only so much someone could take before they broke.

Emma did not want anything to happen to Amy she could not imagine her life without Amy. She did not know if she could carry on. If she had to live without Amy, then she would rather be hanged. Her brain buzzed with all these ideas throughout the night. Emma's brain would not let her sleep. She ran over all the other scenarios that could happen, but ultimately it came down to one outcome, that would definitely happen. They would both be hanged.

Chapter 23

BANG!

Amy heard the noise first. She jumped in her bed. She must have fallen asleep at some point within the night. She didn't remember when she did, it all must have got too much, and exhaustion must have taken over her body.

Amy suddenly felt guilty. She had been sitting in her cot worrying about the noise and not thought once about Emma, who was sat in the cell next door struggling to carry on. Amy could not imagine how Emma was coping with it all. Amy herself was barely coping, so she could not see how Emma was.

Another bang put Amy's thoughts to an end. The monitors were here: that was the only explanation. There was no concept of time within the cells, it was dank and dark no matter the time of day. It was impossible to tell what time it was. Amy presumed it was morning as it sounded as though the monitors were having a briefing within the room opposite. Her time being a monitor had taught her that the number of mumbling monotonous voices could only mean that the monitors were talking about something that they did not want to be discussing.

They could only be discussing their hangings. This was something that the monitors did not enjoy doing. They were people after all. Amy was not filled with sympathy for the monitors at this point. She was more concerned about the fact that the love of her life was trapped in the cell next door and there was nothing that she could do about it. How was she going to convince these people to let Emma go? Amy had come to the conclusion that she could not save them both, but she did have the ability to save Emma.

Amy had been formulating this plan within the night. She was going to speak to her father and see if she could organise something to happen so that Emma could go free. She could not let Emma hang in two days' time. She had to make sure that she did something about this.

"All prisoners report to the front of their cells!"

The pre-recorded robotic voice was chilling. It sent chills through Amy's spine. This could only mean that interviewing day was here. Interviewing day was something that Amy had been spoken through within her training, she knew how it all worked but it was different being on the receiving end of it all. Amy had never had much to do with the headquarters of the monitors. She was always going to be involved in the higher ranks and be the one on the front line, so she had missed out on the basic training within the headquarters.

Amy saw this as putting her at a disadvantage within this situation. She did not know how to deal with this. She did not know how to help the woman that she loved as she stood trapped within cell next door. Amy felt helpless. There was nothing she could do.

The monitors walked down the dingy corridor in formation. They were like a pride of lions, weighing up their prey and preparing to take them down. Amy was scared, she knew that she was the prey. She knew that she was the one that the monitors wanted. They did not want Emma, not really. They wanted her, the perpetrator. Amy could only hope that she was right, she could not risk Emma's life.

She could not live with the idea that she had put Emma's life in danger. This was all her, she had been the first to come up with this crazy idea. She was the one who had confessed her love first. She was the one who had gone through with it. It was because of Amy that these two girls faced the issues that they were facing right now. It was all Amy's fault.

Amy saw the monitors walking towards her cell. She could barely breathe with the fear. What was she going to do? What was she going to say? She couldn't cope with the idea of what was happening. She was going to have to come up with a plan to get to her father. He was now her only chance of getting Emma out of this hell hole. But it was not her that the monitors wanted. They walked straight past her cell and towards Emma. Amy screamed.

"No please, interview me. She isn't strong enough to do this! Please, interview me, I'm begging you!"

The desperation in her voice was evident. Amy knew that by showing her weakness she had made herself vulnerable, but there was nothing else that she could do. How else was she going to get them to listen. They couldn't interview Emma first, not now. It would kill her. She would not be able to deal with it all.

Amy sat and watched helplessly as Emma was dragged out of her cell. She looked nothing like herself. All the life had been sucked out of her by this horrible place. She was pale and blotchy and looked like all her blood had drained out of her body. How did this place affect people in this way? It had a way of sucking all the life out of everything that came near it. Especially those that were stuck in there night and day. Amy gasped when she saw Emma's frail frame. She saw what she was being reduced to. She knew she had to do something to make this craziness end. How was she going to help Emma? How could she make all this nonsense go away?

They lead Emma like a dog, clicking onto the chain around her neck to keep hold of her. How could they be so cruel to another living thing. Amy was almost embarrassed when she thought about all the years, she had put into training to be one of these people. Why had she done it? Why had she put herself through it all? That was a question that she could not answer.

As Emma disappeared behind the large steel door and Amy heard the clink of the lock, she knew that Emma was going to return the shadow of her former self. How was she going to be able to ensure Emma's safety when she was stuck within this stupid cell.

Amy had made her decision. It was how she was going to make it happen. She had to do something drastic. Something that would make her father come and see her. That was all she needed. She needed her father. He was the one man within Baskerville that could make this all go away. He could turn it all into a terrible dream. He could make it all okay.

Chapter 24

Emma wasn't fully aware of what was happening when she was brought into the interview room. She had been woozy ever since she got into her cell. She wasn't sure if they had given her something to stop her from crying, because at this moment she felt nothing. There was no emotion running through her veins like normal. There was just nothing: only emptiness.

The interview room was cold, not just in temperature. It was clear that bad things happened here. How bad, Emma was sure she would soon find out.

The walls were padded in a medical like green giving the sense of an operating theatre. The floor was made up of cold and dank tiles. Much like the ones in the cells. They were also wet, like they had recently been hosed down. The water glistened in the dark orange light that was being emitted by the small light bulb hanging from the ceiling in the centre of the room.

There were no windows within this room, giving the impression that what happened here was not fit for the public to see. This was the interview room that Emma and Amy had both studied within monitor school. This was the room where they decided if you were guilty or not, by any means necessary.

Emma was thrown onto the chair that was sitting in the middle of the room. It was slightly to the left of the light which gave it an even eerier feel. Emma still could not feel anything. She was beginning to get concerned.

"I just need to give you this before we can interview you, Emma. Something to take the edge off the sedation."

Emma knew she did not feel right. The bastards had been sedating her the whole time she had been here. There was a part of her that did not want the edge taking off. She had been quite happy being empty. It had helped her cope.

The monitor strapped Emma's arm into the chair and stuck the needle in so far that Emma was sure it was going to come through on the other side. It was instant. As soon as she felt the cold of the liquid seeping through her veins, her whole outlook changed. She was suddenly aware of everything that was going on. She wanted to scream for help. To let someone, know that she was trapped here. But then she remembered that no one would come. She was a criminal in the monitors' minds, and they were going to prove it.

"Now you look more with us. So…could you describe your relationship with Miss Cleave to us?"

It was an innocent question, but the monitor put it across in such a way that made it sound very sinister.

There had to be a certain type of monitor working in the cells. The ones that got the sadistic pleasure out of making someone else feel pain. They were the type of people that you did not want to be out of the governments control as they would just go wild. Not even the threat of Baskerville's council could keep these in check, and it was one of these exact people that stood before Emma as she thought about how she was going to answer that very open question.

"She's my very good friend. I have known her since monitor school, we did the school together and then we have been friends ever since. I go to her house to have dinner with her and her partner quite frequently."

Emma was pleased with her response. She had made it sound like an innocent relationship. Like there was nothing untowardly going on. She thought that she had been very convincing.

"I am going to ask you again, and this time I want the truth!"

He was becoming agitated, and Emma had a feeling that this would end badly for her, but she was sticking to her story. She had planned what she had to say, and she knew how she was going to say it. This was her only chance at living. She had to persuade this person that she was purely friends with Amy and nothing else. She would just have to take the punishment and no matter what was thrown her way, she was going to have to stick to her story.

The monitor tightened the fastenings around Emma so that she could not move away from the chair and it was then that he sent the electricity pulsing through her body. The charge of what felt like a thousand fire bolts straight through Emma's body. It had caught Emma off guard. She was not expecting this much at first, she thought it would be built up.

As Emma writhed and kicked out at the electricity, the monitor let out a sadistic laugh. He was clearly enjoying this far more than he should and as Emma's body began to shake, he turned it off.

Once the electricity had stopped there was an eerie silence, Emma had never felt pain like that before. It was the most deep and intense pain that she had ever felt in her life, but she was still not going to give up and tell them all her secrets she was not giving up because of some simple electricity.

"As my previous comment, we are simply very good friends."

Emma was not for budging. There was nothing that this man could do to her that would make her give Amy up. She would die if she had to, but she was not going to give up the love of her life.

The monitor was circling her like a vulture waiting for her to cave. Emma could see in his eyes that he was enjoying this. She had the feeling that she had been an any means necessary kind of case, which will have excited the monitor.

"So, you're too tough for the electric huh? I know something even more fun that we can try if you're up for it?"

As he said this, he pulled a razor blade out of his pocket.

"One small nick on the neck is all it would take to finish you…I'd be able to sit and watch the blood drain out of your body slowly. Watch you turn from pink to purple to blue to white. I'd be able to watch the light disappear from your eyes. But do you know what the best bit would be? I'd be able to tell your girlfriend that you were dead!"

Emma knew that he was right. If she didn't give him some information, all of those things would become true. He would be able to do all of those things and she did not want to leave this cell in a body bag. She wanted to fight this with Amy. She wanted to show the world that you can get through anything.

The monitor was laughing again. Almost like a cackle of excitement as he drew the blade.

The first cut was hardest. It went deep into her thigh and the blood was pouring. Thick and red, like a volcano, it showed no signs of stopping. Emma was beginning to think that he had nicked the vein. He carried on, cutting into her thigh like she was simply a piece of meat ready for the butchers. The pain was immense, but Emma could get through it. She was tougher than people thought.

"Every cut is going to be deeper, until you tell me the truth. If I were you, I would tell me the truth now? It would be easier for both of us. And it would save on a lot of clearing up."

Emma refused. She was not going to breathe a word. She would be quite until he had given up.

The monitor began to play with the controls on the panel next to him and Emma began to feel her arms lifting. She had been put into a cinch without realising. First arms then her torso and then her legs followed, until she was simply dangling from the ceiling via her wrists. Emma was helpless in this state. She could not defend herself. The monitor was winning. Emma began writhing within the constraints, trying desperately to get free, but the monitor was simply overpowering her.

Another cut, straight down her stomach. Emma could still feel the blood pouring out of her. She could not see how much more blood she had to lose. The clean tiles that had once stood under her were now splattered with blood stains and contained a pool of blood that could only be Emma's.

Emma was now weak from the assault and did not know if she had any more cards to play. She didn't know how she could escape from this without telling the truth. It was impossible. She would not be able to do it. This was how she was going to die. She was going to die in a pool of her own blood hanging from the ceiling.

"Any more comments to add, or shall we carry on?" The monitor chuckled.

The fact that he was enjoying this really did concern Emma. He should not be getting that excited over torturing another human life.

He reached over to the table next to him and pulled out an iron poker. This poker was unlike any poker Emma had seen before. It was almost magical, had it been in other circumstances. Emma knew that this would be the one for her. She had already become dizzy from the loss of blood, her brain had gone foggy, and she didn't know if she would be able to take anymore from him.

"So, this is your last chance to tell me. What kind of relationship do you have with Miss Cleave? I would think over your answer very carefully before you answer as this could be the difference between life or death."

Emma couldn't move, she could barely speak. Her brain was starting to fog, and she was struggling to breathe. Even if she had wanted to tell the monitor the truth, she was not sure that she could put two words together without running out of oxygen. She was unable to do anything, she had been beaten. She knew it would happen but she did not think it would happen like this!

The monitor took her silence as obstinance rather than crying for help and began to warm up the poker in the open flame.

"You do realise that once this goes onto your skin, everyone will know forever that you didn't answer the questions that were being asked of you!"

His face told Emma all that she needed to know. Even if she did come clean at this point, she would still be getting branded. The monitor had decided that she deserved it, and nothing was going to change that right now.

Underneath all the chaos Emma was silently preparing herself for the pain. She knew that this would be the worst pain that she had ever encountered. The government had made the brand this way. They had made it with a special iron that has a higher burning temperature than anything else on the planet. This means that in the flame, it can get up to temperatures beyond imagination. This was what it was designed for.

Those who did not comply. This was the last resort. Not only would it be the worst pain that a human can go through, but you would have that mark on you for the rest of your life. They also didn't put it somewhere that could be easily hidden. The brand was placed just below your right ear and down your neck. Where the skin was the most sensitive. One for the pain, and two, for the threat.

"Okay, one more time. What is your relationship with Miss Cleave?"

The monitor was almost cheering under his breath as he said those words. Almost begging her not to say anything, begging for permission to put the brand on her neck. Emma was unable to respond, she had become weaker and more vulnerable as the time had passed and she was dropping in and out of consciousness like a yoyo. She wanted to respond, she wanted to tell him to stop and phone for an ambulance, but there was just no point. He wasn't going to anyway.

The brand had become bright red under the flame. Not the orange that you imagine when you think of hot metal. This had gone way beyond that. The brand was scarlet red with the heat that it was giving off. Emma could just about make it out in her disappearing vision, and the last thing she saw as she passed out was the monitors grin as he pushed the brand onto her neck.

Chapter 25

Amy was sitting, huddled up, in the corner of her cell when she heard it.

The bloodcurdling scream of Emma.

She jumped up, out of the corner of the room. She knew it was her, it couldn't be anyone else. No one else could have that effect on her. Amy knew who the scream belonged to and it caused her unknown pain. Pain that was mixed with helplessness as there was nothing she could do.

"YOU BASTARDS, YOU BASTARDS!"

Amy had been taken over by some sort of other energy. She knew that the monitors were to blame, but she knew that there was someone else that was to blame, someone who had taken charge of all of this and someone who Amy knew very well.

She had to get to her dad.

Her dad would be able to fix all this, he would be able to stop the monitors from doing this and most importantly let them go!

Suddenly there was a clink from the bottom of the corridor, Amy knew that this was Emma being returned to her cell after the questioning. She knew that she had one chance to reassure her that everything was going to be okay. Amy ran to the front of her cell ready to see Emma walk back to her cell, but there was no Emma. The monitor came out, but he was alone.

"I think I might have pushed it a bit hard with this one Sarge. She just wasn't up to it."

Amy felt the strength in her legs disappear. She couldn't live like this; she couldn't live without her. She didn't know what she would do without her.

All of Amy's insides were churning as she stood and stared at the door, but there was no one coming. That was it. There was only the monitor coming out of that room. There was no sign of Emma.

Amy could only sit and watch as four men in white coats went into the room, what they brought out was something that Amy was not ready to see.

The four men came out with something that looked like a body led on the bed. As they wheeled her up the aisle towards the door out of the cells, Amy let out a scream. She was unable to control herself when the bed was wheeled past her cell. She looked over the lifeless body that was being wheeled past her. The shadow of her love. Emma was white, like a ghost, only worse as it was like her ghost had already left her. Amy stretched her hand through the bars and was able to brush her fingers down Emma's arm. It was cold as ice.

It was this that brought the reality of it all to focus for Amy.

A wave of misery was rushing through Amy, like a cold breeze on a winter's day. She didn't know what emotions she was feeling right now. All she knew was that she did want to live on this earth if she had to live without Emma. She could not bring herself to imagine what life would be like without her. How she would cope, how she would carry on living.

Amy let her emotions out the only way she knew how. She threw herself around the cell like she was demented. Screaming Emma's name, knowing there would be no reply. The guards let her carry on. It was like they knew that they had taken this too far. They knew that they could not do anything to help this girl as they had already ruined her. They had ruined everything about her and there was nothing that they could do to make it any better.

Hours had passed before Amy ran out of steam. She led on the bed gasping for air. She had been screaming and crying and everything in between. She did not know how she was going to carry on without Emma, but she knew that it was something that she was going to have to deal with. She needed to get out of the cell. She needed to do something in Emma's memory to show her that she would not give up. Just because Emma had been taken did not mean that Amy was going to give up. She was not going to let this all be for nothing. She was going to make a change. She was going to change Baskerville forever!

After what seemed like days had passed, the monitors began to interact with Amy a little more, Amy did not recede though. She would not speak to those who had murdered Emma in cold blood. There was no need for this to become so violent so soon: there was no need for Emma to have lost her life, purely because she was gay. Amy had formulated a plan in her head, and she was going to carry it out, for Emma.

"Amy, you are needed in the interview room. Please stand at the back of the cell with your arms up. The monitor will cuff you and you will be escorted there. If you come quietly, nothing bad will happen."

This was it! This was Amy's interview. This was her chance to start her plan. She didn't know how she was going to make it work and it would take a lot of good luck and chance, but she was going to try. She had to do something. She refused to stand on the stage in front of the whole town while they cheered. She had to put a stop to this!

The monitor came round the back of her and placed her wrists within the constraints. She would comply with what they wanted for a time. It was the only way that she could get this plan into action. It would only happen if they thought she was doing as she was told.

Amy was lead down the alley and through the door at the bottom. She entered the interview room and saw the horror that it encased. She had seen the interview room when she had been training but it was a very different sight when you knew that it was all there for you. The monitor threw her down into the chair and two others strapped her into it.

"You have one chance for every question to give us the correct answer. Failure to comply will not work out well for you. I suggest you answer every question correctly first time and then no one needs to get hurt."

The seriousness of his voice scared Amy a little. What would she be punished for? She was not going to sit still and comply with this monster. If they wanted her to do as she was told, they would have to do better than an electric chair!

The monitor grabbed the piece of paper, which Amy presumed had the questions written on it. She knew that she was not going to give them the answers that they wanted. She refused to give in. She was not going to give them an excuse. She had to speak to her father if she was going to change any of this. She had to make him understand that this was insane. People being murdered purely for the person they love; it was breaking so many human rights.

The monitor read the first line and prepared himself. This was probably the biggest moment of his career, Amy almost felt sorry for him that it was going to go so badly. He could do whatever he wanted to her; she was not going to give him any information.

"Amy what is your relationship with Emma?"

It was a simple question. A question that could change Amy's life forever though. Amy refused to conform and give them the answer that they were longing for. She had already decided that she was going to give them the answers that they wanted. She had already decided what she was going to do.

"I'm not giving any answers until I have seen my father, Boris Cleave. Get him for me and I will tell you everything I know, but until then I will not speak!"

Amy was strong in her convictions she knew that if she could wait out the monitors, they would get bored and give in, but it was whether she would be able to deal with the punishments that she was sure they had in store for her.

"You have had your chance, but I am feeling charitable. So, I will ask you again. What was the relationship like?"

The monitor spoke with an edge of irritation. He was becoming annoyed. He knew that he had to get the information from Amy without taking it too far. He had seen what had happened to the other monitor that had interviewed Emma. He did not want to end up like that. He knew he had to gain the information without hurting Amy too much.

Amy knew this.

"No comment," she replied, calmly.

Chapter 26

The pain from the chair was something that could not be described. As the electricity rushed through Amy's body, she lost all control of herself. She could not stand strong against the monitors; she could not stand at all. Her brain was fighting the current but with little success she had to give in. As soon as she gave in the electric stopped.

"See I am not so unreasonable. You comply and no one must get hurt. It is very simple. Answer the questions and you leave here unscathed."

The monitor was almost chuckling. The fact that he was enjoying this was annoying Amy even more. She did not want to give him the satisfaction, but there was little that she could do.

"One more chance, what was your relationship?"

Amy knew that she could not push it too much further. She knew that she had pushed it too far as it was. This was the law in Baskerville, and she would have to adhere to it or risked being hanged. She had already pushed the boundaries on the monitors, and she did not want to push them too much further, but she had to do something. This was not how she was going to go down.

"One more chance, get my dad!"

The monitor knew he was pushing it, but he refused to cave. He knew he had to get the information out of her somehow.

He began to lower the chains from the ceiling and Amy knew what happened with those chains. As the chains lowered Amy began to feel a little scared. She knew that this was the last stage of the interrogation process and what, she could only imagine, was the reason that the love of her life had left this room in a body bag.

Once the chains were lowered the monitor attached Amy's arms into the shackles. His smug look knocked Amy sick. How could someone gain so much pleasure out of watching other people suffer? These people were animals and there was nothing more to it. They were horrible. But Amy was not going to give in to them. She had to stay strong. She was now doing this for Emma.

She had to show them that she was stronger than them, no matter what they threw at her, she was going to stand against it and prove that it was not right what they were doing, and it needed to change. If she could just hold on longer than the monitor, her plan would come into action.

The monitor was almost grinning as he pressed the button that lifted Amy up out of the chair. The chains were clinking in a manner that was almost eerie. Amy had swallowed all her fear and was ready to show the monitor that he could not hurt her. If she did not react, then he would not get the satisfaction of her reaction and that was how she planned to play it. She would not give him the satisfaction of unnerving her. That was not happening.

Before Amy had a chance to think anything through, she was hanging from the ceiling. The chair had been removed and she could only hang there.

The monitor looked over her as if she was a piece of meat. Deciding which part of her he should start with. Amy was ready for him though. She was not going to go down without a fight.

The monitor walked towards her with the standard issue knife that was given to all monitors for situations exactly like these.

"In order to do this, we need to make sure you know the rules. Give me the correct answer and I will let you down from here. Give me the wrong answer and you will gain a cut. Every time you lie, you will gain another cut. The choice is yours. Do you understand?"

Amy was unsure what to do at this point. She knew that she needed to see her father but without the monitor summoning him she would never be able to gain access to him. Boris was the only one who could put a stop to this and to help Amy get out of this problem.

"Can we please just speak to my father? Once I can speak to him, we can sort all this out."

She knew that she was asking for the impossible and the chances of them ringing him were very low, but she had to keep trying. Boris was the only one who would be able to sort this out. He was the one who had the power to explain to the monitors that they had to stop this torture.

The monitor sat and looked at Amy dead in the eye. Amy knew that she had gone too far. She knew that she should not have asked again. But she had and she would have to live with the consequences of that. He slowly pulled out the knife, Amy knew what was going to happen next. She knew that she was going to be given the first cut. She knew that this was it for her. She tensed her muscles, getting ready for the blow.

The blow was hot. Amy could feel the heat running through her body. It was not just where the knife had cut, the heat ran all through her body. Amy knew that there were many more to come and she would have to prepare for more of that searing pain. She would have to prepare herself for that pain. She could not show any weakness within this interrogation. That was what the monitors wanted.

The monitor had a slight smile on his face as the opportunity arose for the second cut. But, before the knife could be sunk into her a red light appeared on the wall coupled with a computerised voice announcing there was someone at the door.

All the hope that Amy had within her has mustered to the surface. Could this be her father? Could he have finally come to save her? This could be it for Amy. She could be about to be free from the torment that was happening within her life.

Chapter 27

Amy could tell that the monitor was not happy that he had been disturbed. It was clear that he was gaining a lot of pleasure in what he was about to do. He was at a disadvantage though, Amy was numb. She did not care what happened to her now. She had nothing to live for anymore. She had seen the love of her life be wheeled out of this chamber; she had nothing to fight for. There was nothing else that she wanted but for her to live happily with the woman of her dreams and that was all gone now. None of that was possible anymore.

The beep of the door was piercing. It attacked Amy's ears like a viper, sending a searing pain through her whole head.

"Boris Cleave is about to enter the room, please stop all procedures and stand at the side of the room. Leave the prisoner where they are but make sure that all restrains are fastened tightly. Thankyou."

How could something so cruel be said so calmly, like a simple announcement within a supermarket?

The monitor stepped away from Amy and moved to the side of the room. He knew that this was the highest rated monitor that was about to enter the room, but this was unprecedented. People did not enter the room during the torture stage. It was something that just did not happen.

Amy could see it on his face that he was unsure as to what he had done wrong. She could see the panic within his face as he presumed that this was all because of him. Amy knew different though, she knew that her father was here to see her. She just did not know whether this was a good thing or not.

There was a loud clunk, that could only mean that the door had been opened. The creak of the rusty hinges screamed as the door was prised open. Boris Cleave filled the gap of light within the opening and proceeded into the room. Amy could feel the tension grow within the room as her father walked up to her. The monitor did not know what to do. This was something that did not happen and something that you were not trained to deal with. He suddenly looked very uncomfortable.

"I would like some time alone with my daughter now please, could you please wait outside so that we can talk privately."

It was worded like a question, but it was not anything of the sort. The monitor nearly ran out of the room, wanting to get out of there as soon as possible. He did not want to be within that situation, he wanted to get out. He did not need telling twice when it came to leaving the room.

The door shut with a bang.

There was only Amy and Boris left within the room and Amy could feel the tension growing as Boris walked over to her hanging by her wrists.

"Never did I think that I would have to come and visit my daughter within this chamber. I thought that I had brought you up better that this. I thought that I had shared values with you and told you how to live your life according to the rules of this sacred town. I don't know what you want me to say to you other than how disappointed I am in you."

Amy didn't know how to react. She thought that her father was her knight, but it was clear that he was not here to rescue her. That small piece of hope within Amy disappeared, like the tiny flame that she had managed to nurture had suddenly gone out. All she had left was the small flakes of smoke that drifted around what was once there.

"Dad, I don't know what you want me to say. I don't even understand why I am here. I don't see why I am being tortured because of the person that I love. I just don't think it is fair!"

Amy knew that was not what she was supposed to say. She knew that this was not something that her father wanted to hear. But she had said it now, it was too late. The words had already come out of her mouth. She had told her dad that she was in love with her. This was the first time she had used those words.

This was the first time Boris would realise just how serious the situation is. This was the first time that Boris would realise that his daughter really was in love with this woman and there was nothing that could be done about it.

Boris took a moment. Amy could see that he was unsure what he was going to say next. He did not know what to say to her to make this better and Amy could see this. Amy could see the anger within his face. She could see that he was not happy about the situation.

135

"I don't know what to say to you really, I don't know what to do to make this better. I don't think I can do anything in order to help you. We simply have to let the law take its course, I am afraid."

That was it. He had given up on her. Amy didn't know what to think. Her own dad had given up on her. Her own dad had given her to the law. He did not care. At least that was how it felt.

"Dad please, I need you to do something. Don't help me that is fine, but I want to know about Emma. Dad please. Just find out if she is okay for me. I need to know that what I saw isn't true. Please."

Amy could hear the desperation in her voice which was something that she did not want to put across to her father. She did not want him to know how desperate she was and how much she needed to know that Emma was okay. But this was something that she needed to know. She needed to know whether she needed to fight or not, whether it was worth her time or whether she should just give up now.

"Amy that girl is not your main concern right now. You need to be thinking about yourself and how you are going to get out of this mess. You need to be thinking about how you are going to carry on with life after this, if there even is a life after this. You are on the list for slaughter you know that don't you? I don't even know if I will be able to overthrow it at this point. This is out of my hands."

"The case has already been taken to the court, they are simply waiting for your answers and then it will be finished. Think wisely about what you say to the monitors. They are looking for a way to catch you out. It is like they want you dead. This is the biggest case they have had in years, and they are going to enjoy it so please make sure that you are careful about what you say to them. Please."

Amy could tell that he was serious, but she did not have any words for what was being said to her. She was not going to be careful about what she said to them, and she was certainly not going to show any weakness to them. She would stay strong and not give them the satisfaction of showing any sign of being hurt. That would make it too easy for them.

She was going to make her point by slipping away silently. She would not say another word until someone told her about Emma. She needed to know that what she had seen was not true. She needed to know that her one true love was okay and that there was still a chance that they could get on with their lives together.

Amy thought long and hard before replying to her father. She knew that he would be thinking about what her strategy was and he was ready to give her the tips. He could not help her physically, but he could give her some ideas.

"I'm done fighting. I can't carry on fighting until I know that I have something to fight for. I am not saying another word until I know what happened to Emma. Could you tell me please, you must know? Please Dad just do this one thing for me."

Boris did not know what to say. His body had gone into some form of weird protective state. He did not know whether to run, hide or cry. He just wanted his little girl to do well in the world that was all. He did not understand what he had done wrong with her. He must have done something, but the idea of having to tell her that her dear friend would not be coming back was a hard thing to do for any father, even one who did not believe in the relationship at all.

"Amy, baby, Emma isn't coming back to Baskerville. She's gone, she isn't coming back."

It was like the clocks had stopped…

Amy was trying to gather her thoughts and calm herself down but being tied to the ceiling by her hands seems to only exaggerate the feeling of sadness that she had within her heart. It had all been for nothing, everything she was fighting for was for nothing. She had an incline that something had happened, and that Emma was not okay, but this was final.

It was from her dad. She had suffered at the hands of the monitors, in a way that she could never imagine. Amy would never see her again, she would never touch her again, she would never feel her soft skin against her own. She was gone.

If it was not for the fact that Amy was tied to the ceiling via ropes, Amy was sure she would have fallen. Her legs simply gave way, and it was like all the fight that was left in her had suddenly disappeared. She had nothing left, nothing that she wanted to fight for. She didn't have any reason left in the world other than to give up. That was it, she had given up. It took a while for her to realise but she knew it was final. Where a world of opportunity had once stood; there was just nothing.

Chapter 28

As the sun rose over the town of Baskerville, it was clear that something big was happening on this day. It was clear that this was going to be a big day in the history of Baskerville. The whole town knew it and you could sense it within the streets. It was early, really early, but the streets were bustling. There were people walking around like it was the middle of the day.

This was because it was the day of the hanging. Everyone had the day off work to come and watch it. People seemed excited, which was almost sad. The idea that someone could be excited about another person losing their life was something that was sad about Baskerville. It was what let the town down when it came to the values of the people there.

Amy was sitting in her holding cell. Simply waiting. She could not do anything more or say any more, there was simply no point. She was almost looking forward to the end. It would mean that she would be able to leave this cruel world and find the woman of her dreams. It meant that her and Emma would be able to be together after all, just not in the way that she had imagined.

The sound of the town was echoing down the hall into Amy's cell. She didn't know how many people had come to see her, but it was sad to think that there was anyone. Amy was hoping that no one would come and that they would show a little compassion to her considering her heritage and the fact that her father was the leader of the monitors. This did not seem to be the case. They were not interested in sparing her. All they wanted was another hanging. They did not mind how they got it.

There was a loud clunk at the door to the cell. Amy jumped. She knew this was the time and, although she had been romanticising about it, she was very nervous about the idea that this would be the last few minutes of her life. The last time that her dad would say her name, and the last time her mum would see her.

She knew that she could not cry, she was not even sure if she had the strength to cry within her. She was broken. Compared to how she had felt when she was with Emma, before all this craziness had begun, she was so happy, nothing could have brought her down.

The monitor was looking her up and down, he knew that she was going to be hung. He knew that this was the last time that he would see her, but it did not seem real. It did not seem real that there was going to be an actual hanging in Baskerville. Even the monitors were confused, hangings were so rare. What had this person done?

Amy could feel his eyes looking her up and down, thinking about what she had done. She couldn't deal with the shame. Why had her father let this happen to her? Why had he not stopped it? Amy had hoped that if anyone would be able to finish this trauma it would have been him. But that dream was long finished. She had seen her father and he had seen her, but still he did nothing.

Whether or not that was a choice that he had made or whether there really was nothing that he could have done was something that Amy was trying not to think about. She didn't want to know if her dad had betrayed her on purpose or if he truly was telling the truth and there was nothing more that could be done.

Amy had a sudden wave of fear come over her. She was not going to be able to escape from this. This was it. This was the end of her life. All Amy could think about was getting back to Emma. That was all she had to look forward too now. She had to die, if she died then she would be able to be with Emma in the afterlife and life forever together.

As the walk to the stocks seemed to become longer Amy had time to really think about what she was doing. This would give her the time to really think about her life and what she had done with it. It would give her the time to be grateful of everything that she had in her life and everyone that had been a part of it.

The walk seemed to go on forever. It seemed to be the longest walk that Amy had ever gone on. She never remembered the walk being that long before. She had never thought about what they would be thinking when they were walking down that bridge. It was hell.

As she arrived at the stairs, she could hear the audience shouting her name. She could hear the hate within their shouts. It was almost unbelievable that a whole town could group together to hate someone so profusely when they had no idea really what had gone on. This just showed the power of the rules within this poisoned society. It just showed what a few simple rules could do a community. They had turned on her. She was once respected and sought after and now they hated her. It was fine though, Amy hated them. She hated them all for what they had done to Emma and how they had made her feel throughout this whole epidemic.

As Amy approached the noose, she could see that the whole town had come out to see this. They were not going to miss something like this. It was like they could not miss it even though their brains were telling them that they had do. It was like the town had completely brainwashed them.

Boris Cleave had been relieved of his judge duty because of the circumstances and his second in command stood up to the post. It was up to him to have the final say in whether she was guilty. If someone had got this far, however, it was clear that they were already guaranteed to be hung. There was no point denying it.

"We are all here today to see justice be done for crimes against the state. We are witnessing today, the execution of Amy Cleave for homosexual activity within Baskerville. As you all know this is forbidden and will not be tolerated within this town. That is why, we have decided that she should be put to death."

The town was deathly silent. Not even the birds were tweeting. It was like they knew. They knew that something was happening, something that would change the world forever. The town knew it too. It was clear that today was going to be a big day in the justice system and it would show within the history books.

That was all that Amy wanted. She just wanted them to remember her. She wanted them to know that she had suffered at the hands of the state and that there was no need for this. There was no need for any of this to have happened.

Chapter 29

Amy stepped up onto the step that would be removed when it was time. The noose was placed around her neck, and she was asked to recite the prayer of Baskerville. This was protocol for someone who was facing the hanging. She began slowly, she had lost all emotion. It was like she was sitting watching someone else do all this. She was no longer in her body. She was almost looking forward to that moment of impact when she had to no longer worry about this world and could purely focus on getting back to Emma. They could finally be together once this noose was tied around her neck.

"Clear the stage!"

For a hanging to take place, there could be no one standing on the stage. This was to ensure there were no murder claims from the family of the criminal. Everyone cleared the stage, apart from Amy who simply stood there waiting for the chair to disappear through the hole in the floor.

The crowd had become restless as they knew that they should be supporting this individual who was clearly showing strength against the government, but they just couldn't deny their love of a hanging. They began to count down from ten, almost in a cheery tone which did not match the situation.

Just as the crowd got to eight, and Amy had finally given up all her fight, she felt someone behind her grab her and pull her off the stage. Amy did not have a chance to discover who the person was, she was too busy running with them. They had her hand, and she was struggling to match pace. She had not eaten for several days and was struggling with the lack of energy, she could feel her legs protesting as they hit the ground hard with every step, but they had to carry on. This was the only way that she was going to be free.

The monitors sprung into action. They would not be beaten by a teenage girl and this mystery saviour. All their energy was put into spreading out in order to find the girl and her friend who had embarrassed the monitors and made them look incompetent.

"Get them!"

If there was ever a time where someone sounded the angriest, they had ever been it was now. Boris Cleave had been waiting in the wings. He did not want to be in the public eye while his daughter was about to be hung but he did want to leave the monitors to their own devises. He wanted to make sure that his daughter was caught.

The idea that she could escape would be the end of his career. Everyone would think that he had something to do with it and it was his fault. This was not the case; he did not have anything to do with springing her out like this. He simply had to find out who the person was who had come to her rescue.

Amy had never heard her father sound like that. It was anger and panic mixed. It was a sound that Amy did not want to hear again. It was almost that she did not want to run. She did not want to disobey her father when he was this upset, but it was either disobey him or die. There was no other option. She had to run. She had been fuelled by her rescuer. They had risked everything to save her. She had to give them the credit that they deserved by at least running with them.

Amy followed the figure up through the town, it was deserted as the whole town had gathered at the town centre to watch the hangings. It was perfect really for them to get away.

When they got the edge of town, it was also deserted. There was no one there. The monitors had obviously put all their men at the hanging in case something had happened.

The black figure carried on running. They were not stopping. Amy was following, unsure where they were going. They were running down with the fence, staying as close to it as possible. Until the figure finally stopped. They turned around briefly to see if she was still following them, and it was then that Amy realised who she had been following this whole time. Who her saviour was and how they had come to her rescue just in the nick of time before her whole world collapsed under her?

"Max? Is that you? You have come to save me? Why?"

Amy couldn't believe it. Why had this person come to her rescue when there was so much at stake for him? He was already at risk of a life sentence and now here he was putting his life at risk again for the sake of the cause. Why was he doing this for her? Why did he care so much about her when she could never give him what he wanted? Amy could not understand it, but if he was going to help her escape, she had to do as he said and get out of this crazy town.

There was a hole just to the side of the fence, Amy knew that the fence was electrified and it would definitely be on today as there were now fugitives on the loose. Amy was wary of the fence, as that was how she had been brought up. She was uneasy just being close to the fence, that was without the prospect of going under it.

Max went first and slipped through the fence with ease. He was at the other side and free. He stood next to a pile of dirt shouting for Amy to do the same.

"Amy come on! I don't know how much time we have left before they realise that we are here. Please come on. I don't want you to be caught again!"

There was a genuine pleading in his voice that startled Amy. He really did want her to survive this. He was not just doing this because he was nice, he really did want her to survive and get away.

Amy leapt into action; she threw herself into the hole like a meercat jumping to safety. The tunnel seemed very long to Amy even though it was only a couple of foot. She felt like she had been underground for an age before she resurfaced on the other side of the fence!

She couldn't believe it. She was on the other side of the fence. It was so beautiful over here, and the air almost seemed cleaner that it had in Baskerville. How that was possible Amy would never know, but it was what she felt.

"Come on! We need to fill in this hole! They cannot know that we have escaped from Baskerville! They need to stay in the town!"

This clicked Amy back into action. She could not relax yet. She had to cover her tracks before she could settle here. She began pushing the pile of dirt that was next to the hole back into it to try and fill it in. It was slowly working and Amy could see the dirt rise at the other end, within the fence.

When the hole was completely filled in, Max began to run towards the woods. Without thinking Amy followed him. He was her only hope to escape this cruel world.

Chapter 30

Amy couldn't believe it. She was finally free of that cruel, cruel, world.

When she finally got to the woods, she stopped to catch her breath and to let it all sink in. What had just happened? How had she just been freed from that life. It was all over.

"Why have you done this? How have you done this? I just don't understand how you made it possible!"

Amy had too many thoughts running through her brain at this moment. She did not know how to get all her thoughts together. This was something completely new for her. It was something she was not familiar with it at all. Someone had put her life first and had risked their own to preserve hers. This was unfamiliar to Amy. She was not used to this. She had always been loved but there was always something more important than her. Something that would always go above her. This was new. Someone had put her first. Above anything. This was a feeling that Amy did not think was natural.

As they approached the middle of the woods, it became clear that this was the base camp. This was where Amy would be spending some of her nights. There was a big tent and a fire in front of it. It was clear that people had been living here for a long time.

"I know that things don't make a lot of sense right now, but a lot has happened while you were in prison. You were locked away for a long time and something had to be done in order to make sure that we could get you out. You couldn't die for loving someone. That is just wrong, so I came up with a plan and actioned it. You were the last step!"

Amy couldn't believe it. All the time she had been worried about bringing Max into the equation, worrying whether or not she would be able to trust him and here he was saving the day and saving her life.

But there was one thing that Max could not change. Neither of them had been able to save Emma. All of this felt like it was for nothing. There was no need for

Amy to have escaped and there was no need for Max to have put his whole life in danger because now they were outcasts and would have to go and make a name for themselves in the new world. But all of this was futile, for Amy at least, it made no sense doing this now without Emma.

"I have to ask you something Max. Why have you done this? You're ruined now. Your whole life is over, you could have been really happy within Baskerville and just carried on. You might have found the girl for you that would allow you to start a family once I had gone. There was no benefit to you."

Max stopped for a minute and thought about what he was going to say. He looked as though he knew that this question was coming and that he had the answer for it. Amy was stood, poised to know why he had put himself so low down in his priority list and why she was standing there alive when she should have been dead.

"Amy, I have never told you this, but although we are only friends and I respect that we are only friends. We are really good friends, and this is the kind of thing that friends do for each other. I love you, in a friend way and I couldn't bear to see you go through that pain that the government was going to put you through. I couldn't just stand there and do nothing while this was happening. I am just sorry it took me so long. If I had not taken so long to come to the decision, then Emma would not have gone through half the things she had gone through."

That was it. He had said it. He had said her name. Amy could feel her whole body go numb. She didn't want it to be like this, but she knew that she had been avoiding the fact that the last time she had seen her girlfriend she was being wheeled out of the torture chamber like a slab of meat. She didn't want to think about it. She didn't want to bring those tortured memories to the surface again. She felt herself falling, like all her strength had seeped away into the ground, she was a shell. A shell of nothingness that wreaked of desperation.

What was she supposed to do when she had no strength left in her body? How could she possibly function when the woman that she loved had been brutally murdered by the very institution that she worked for. It was all too much for Amy, she could not do this anymore. She had to walk away. This discussion was something that she was not ready for.

It was clear by Max's reaction that he knew that he shouldn't have mentioned Emma quite so soon into the conversation. It was clear that she was not ready to fully understand what was being said to her. She was just a shell of her former self and showed no signs of recognition, never mind emotion. How was Max ever going to repair this girl? He knew he had to, but it was just deciding when and how. That would be the issue now.

Amy knew that she should not be reacting in this way. She had seen Emma be wheeled out; she knew what had happened. She was a victim of the state. Another victim of the state. Amy could not understand what the point of her being removed was, as there was no way she would be able to carry as normal now that she did not have Emma. Amy did not know how to even think about the next step within this escape. There was no point in it. No point in it at all.

"So, what is the plan now then? I know that you have gone to a lot of trouble to get this escape up and running but honestly, without Emma I do not see the point. You should have just left me to die. There is no point in life for me right now."

Amy couldn't understand why the rescue had even gone ahead. The idea that she would now have to carry on with her life without Emma was something that broke her heart. She was trying to think this whole thing through. Would she rather be dead than be without Emma? That was something she would have to think about on her own. This was not something that Max could answer for her. She knew that she had been harsh on Max and it was not his fault, but the plan consisted of getting everyone out, not just her. This mission had been a failure and Amy just couldn't get over that.

Max knew that Amy was frustrated, but he had to make sure that she was sound of mind before he got into the details of the rest of the plan. He knew that she had to be fully committed to the plan before she found out the finer details. This was something he would just have to wait for. This was something that Amy would do in her own time. She had to come to acceptance before Max could move on with the plan, and that was what the base camp was for. Before they went to the little flat that Max had organised within the outskirts of their new town.

"Amy, I get it. It seems like this whole operation has been a failure. But we have done something here. We have done something that could change the world. We have done something that will be in history books for generations, we have escaped Baskerville. Have you heard of someone ever doing that before?"

Max needed to get her to understand that he was right. He knew what they had to do. He knew what the plan was. He also knew something that Amy didn't. Something that would change Amy's whole attitude, but he couldn't tell her yet. It was too soon.

Chapter 31

Amy did not sleep well that night. She had led awake all night thinking about Emma, wondering if she was watching her now and thinking about what she had done. Wondering if Emma knew that Amy was always thinking about her. Amy knew that she was always thinking. There was not a moment when she was not thinking. Emma was always there.

As Amy turned around within her sleeping bag, she saw that Max had prepared her a cup of tea, and some of the biscuits that were issued at home when you were not at home for your breakfast.

This was calming to Amy. Being given what she craved the most was good for her, and it soothed her soul. It made her remember why she loved Max so much and what he had done for her over the past few months. He really had put his life on the line for her. He truly did care about her. This was soothing to Amy and made her feel like there was someone out there for her. In another world, she would have been very happy with Max, but she would never choose him over Emma. She had too much lose.

As the sun began to rise over the horizon, Amy was not sure what the day would bring. She did not know the rest of the plan. She was not even aware that Max had concocted this plan so she was unable to predict what his next move would be. He truly was her hero at this moment in time. There was just one thing missing from this rescues mission, and that was the love of her life.

"Are you up?"

The faint voice that could only be Max's came from the distance. Amy did not know whether to answer or whether to pretend that she was asleep so as not to gain any attention. She did not know if she was ready to start the day, not replying to Max would put off the inevitable and allow her to spend more time reflecting on what the day might bring. She could not imagine living this life alone, without Emma, but she had to figure something out as this was her life now and she would have to get used to it.

With regret, Amy replied and proceeded to exit her tent to see Max. Max already up and dressed and busy cooking something on the fire. Amy did not want to know what animal was on the fire as she was just glad of some food. The biscuits that Max had left her with her cup of tea had barely touched the sides. She was famished. But she was only just realising this now. The day before had been so stress filled that she had not even thought about food once. She was so hungry, and this was only occurring to her now.

The smell of the meat was dancing in Amy's nose. She could not wait to taste it. To have the valuable nutrients within her body. She needed this meal. She needed it to take on the day. Max was stood over the fire, carefully cooking the meat in a manner that meant it did not get charred, like meat does, when cooked on the fire. This was a skill and again Amy was thinking that she could have been so happy with Max if she had never met Emma. She would be a very successful career driven woman, who could come home of an evening to her family. She might even have had some children and made her mother happy. Instead, she had ran away from the state because she had broken such a large rule. She had broken almost the biggest rule within the country.

No homosexual behaviour.

This was all becoming too much for Amy. She had put her whole life on the line and abandoned everything that she knew, for the purpose of living with the person she loved. But this was no longer possible, so Amy could not help but wonder what the point of the whole operation was. But Max seemed to have a plan. He seemed to know what was going on and what that plan was, so Amy would blindly follow him. She trusted him in a way that she could describe, she just knew that this was for the best and she would have to stay with him as he would make everything better.

"So do you have a plan for today?"

Amy was eager to know what the plan was. She needed to know what the idea was going forward. She knew that they could not stay here infinitely. She knew that there must be another section to his plan that would allow to escape properly and be free of this cruel world once and for all.

"Before we go through the plan for today, I need to give you something."

Max routed into his pocket and pulled out a piece of paper. On it was an address and the directions to get there. Amy presumed this was the flat that Max had talked about the night before when discussing the plan vaguely.

"I need you to know where you need to go in case we separated, or something happens to me. We need to be aware that they probably have the monitors looking for us right now. They are not just going to let us walk free. We need to have a plan that will allow us to get out of this alive."

This made Amy nervous. Why was Max preparing for them to be separated? It was like he knew that something bad was going to happen to them and he would not be able to stop it happening. This suggested to Amy that the next phase of the plan would be a dangerous one.

Amy just wasn't ready. She did not want to anyone to put their life on the line for her. She certainly did not want Max to do that for her. She had never done anything for him and here he was putting his whole life on the line to let Amy live her truth. It just showed what a decent person Max was and how Amy was stupid to let him go.

Max was packing everything up when Amy finally started to feel like herself. As she began to think about everything that needed to be done, Max had already packed everything up and was ready to go.

"Where do we go from here then Max? I don't think we can just leave, can we? We have left a trail. They will know that we are here!"

"There isn't a lot we can do about it. They already know that we have escaped, so leaving a campsite won't make a lot of difference when it comes to them tracking us. I think if they were looking for us they would have already found us. We are not that far from the fence. They would have found us by now. I think we just have to accept that they have decided to leave us alone and carry on."

If only Max had known how wrong, he was. If only he had known that they were being watched, it would not have ended to way that it did.

Chapter 32

Snap!

It was like every noise echoed in the woods. Every noise was a threat. Amy was terrified. Max did not say much. It was like he knew that there was nothing that could be said to make it alright. They just carried on walking. They carried on through the woods, trudging through the unforgiving terrain and battling through the loose branches that where clawing at their clothes.

After walking for what seemed like an age, Max heard voices. He threw Amy into the bush and jumped in after her. They could not be caught. They could not be caught by anyone. Max could not risk it, even if they were just locals they could not been seen within this area.

That was when it dawned on Max. There would be no locals this close the fence? The Americans tended to stay as far away from the fence as possible. They did not want to be too close to Baskerville and their nuclear weapons. Max buried himself and Amy even further into the bush. These could only be monitors. There would be no one else this close to the fence. They had come looking for them. He was wrong. He thought that they had been left alone, but it was clear that they had not.

"We can't make too much noise. I think the monitors are following us. That was what that noise was, I am sure. We have to be quiet, please."

Amy was terrified. If the monitors were following them, then it was only a matter of time before they were caught. This was something that worried Amy. She did not want all of this to be for nothing. She wanted them to be able to get out of the hell that was Baskerville, but if the monitors were chasing them then it was becoming less and less likely that they would both get out alive.

There were more noises from the monitors. It seemed that they were getting closer. This was it. Amy could not contain herself any longer. She could not simply sit in the bush and wait to be dragged back into prison. She had to do something to help herself.

"Don't move, please! We need to stay still!"

It was like he knew what she was thinking. It was insane how he did, but he knew. Amy wanted to run, and he was begging her not to. Amy could not see any other option. If she ran, then the monitors would see her and she would stand little chance against them, but if she stayed sitting here then she would be a sitting duck waiting for the monitors to come and shoot them.

"I don't think moving would be advised either."

The croak in the voice sent sudden chills down Amy's spine. She knew what that was. It was not the softness that she was used to from Max.

Now that they had been found, there was little that Amy would be able to do to free herself and carry on with her life now. She was going back to Baskerville. She was going back to the prison that she had to call home. She was going to have to do what the monitors said, otherwise she was going to end up dead.

But while all this was going on, she could not stop thinking about what they had done to Emma and how angry she was at them for everything that they had done.

"I suggest you come with us, back home and we can forget this ever happened. Put your arms out for me please Amy."

It was said in a nice tone, but Amy could tell it was not supposed to be. The monitor was lowering the hand cuffs onto her arms when Max came to the rescue.

Amy didn't know where he had got the courage from, or where he had found the strength, but it was clear that he was mad, and this madness had created brute strength.

To this day Amy cannot fully recall what happened within the two short minutes that were between Max coming to her rescue and Max falling, but something happened. Something dreadful.

All Amy could remember was screaming. Screaming for her life. Screaming for Max and in the end, Amy was sure she could recall screaming for Emma.

She was running, running until she couldn't run any more. Amy didn't know where she was running or even if she would get there, but she was running. She couldn't even imagine what might happen after the next minute. She did not have the faith that she would ever actually get out of this. She did not think she would ever stop running. It was like she was stuck in the vortex of her mind, and she was unable to escape. Her own prisoner, locked in her mind.

As Amy woke up, she was dripping with sweat. She knew that she must have had a bad dream, but she had never had a dream like that before.

It was only when she realised where she was.

She was not where she had started. She was in another part of the woods. She was somewhere completely different to what she was used to. She had not been to this part of the woods before. Was that all the dream? Or had the monitors really found her?

It was only then, as Amy began to wake up fully that she started to remember what had happened during the events of her dream. She had lost Max. She had lost her way. But most importantly, she did not know what the next step was. She did not know where it was that Max was taking her after the woods. It was that plan that was going to bring her to safety. The plan that was now gone.

The events of the past few hours hit Amy like a rock to the stomach. All the images that her brain had stored from the past few hours were playing in her brain like a reel.

She paused.

She had lost the monitors, she had lost Max and more importantly, she had lost Emma. She had lost everything. Everything that had ever been good in her life. It was gone. There was nothing left for her to live for.

All the events were coming back to her now. She was starting to understand what had happened. She was starting to understand what had happened over the past few hours. She was starting to understand what it was that had happened to her, and most importantly what had happened to Max, what they had done to him.

The break of the twig was what had alerted Amy and Max to the fact that they were being followed. They had jumped into the hedge, but it was no use. It was no use as the monitors had found them. They had finished the grand search and had realised that they had finally found the person that they were looking for.

Amy had ran. She had ran for her life. She ran and ran and just kept running. She was running till the point that she had forgotten why she was running. Amy had only come to her senses when she was far away. So far away that she did not even recognise the woods. She did not even recognise the type of scenery that she was looking at. It was all different. She was so far from Baskerville. So far it hurt.

There was one thing that stood out to her though. There was one thing missing. One thing that she had set off with but was no longer there. Max.

She could not think about what had happened to him. Maybe he had got away, Amy did not know. She could only hope that he was free now. Free from the monitors or free from her. Amy was not sure which, she only wished that he was free.

As she came to her senses she started to panic. What would she do without Max? How would she carry on without him? This had all been his plan. It had been his great idea and his way out of here. That was why he was here. He had risked his life to ensure that Amy and Emma would be safe and that was all futile now. It had all been a waste of time, as now Emma was not safe and Amy had lost Max.

Amy was at a loss. She did not know what to do!

Chapter 33

If anyone was going to overthrow Baskerville it was going to be Amy Cleave.

That was what people had said. That was what people had believed when the news of her homosexual tendencies had been released to the public. For a moment, she thought there was going to be real change. An actual chance for her to fully understand what her purpose was on this earth. Unfortunately, it was not to be. She had simply ran. Ran away from the problems. She had not solved any of them.

Amy was wandering. Wandering through the woods without a purpose. She did not have any fight left in her. It had all gone. Disappeared like everyone who had come on this journey with her. Everyone who had ever believed in her and anyone who had ever given her a chance.

She was numb to all this though. No emotion was present within Amy at this moment. She felt nothing. She was empty.

As she walked, she heard a strange noise, almost like a whimpering. She jumped into the nearby bushes.

She knew that it was pointless. It did not sound like a monitor. It sounded more like an injured animal. An injured animal who was desperate for help.

Amy came out from the bushes. She knew that this thing was not going to get her. She could tell from the noise it was making, it was injured. She crept towards the bush where the noise was coming from. She was cautious but inviting. She did not want to scare the animal, and she was keen to save it. She had to do something worthy today to make up for the lives that she had wasted in the past few days.

As Amy got closer, she began to think that she recognised the noise. That she knew what animal would be able to create that noise. It was like she knew the animal that was making the noise. Amy couldn't understand how this was possible, so she carried on regardless. This noise could be anything, but she determined to help it. She had to make sure that this animal was okay. She had to make sure that everything sorted.

She slowly approached the bushes. She could hear it whimpering and could see the blood that was creeping from underneath the bushes. This was going to be something bad; Amy could feel it. As she got closer to the bushes Amy was preparing for something bad. She knew that she was going to see something bad. She was just going to have to deal with.

She walked closer to the bushes, and as she reached over to move the twigs, she suddenly realised she was shaking. It was like her mind already knew what she was going to discover.

She moved the twigs to the side to discover what was creating the noise. To her horror she discovered Max, laying there. Bleeding profusely out of his neck. The monitors must have caught up with him while he was running away. That was the only explanation for what Amy was looking at.

"Amy, you need to run. They are still around I can feel them. You need to run now! Please. Leave me, I already dead. Just run away. Get to the small oak tree, there is a map in there. A map that will lead you to safety! Please Amy, run!"

Amy could tell by the way that Max was talking that he did not have long before he had lost too much blood. She tried to argue with him, but before she could, he was gone.

All Amy wanted to do was scream. Scream so loud that everyone would hear her, everyone would know what had happened! But she knew that she had to be quiet. She knew that no one could know that she was here. She slowly moved towards Max and gave him a kiss on the cheek. She would leave now and find the small oak tree that he had mentioned. This would be the way in which she would help Max. She would go along with the plan that he had made for her all along. She would find the oak tree and find the directions to the safe house. That would be her last act for Max. She would put all his hard work to use. She did not want his life to be wasted. It was too precious for that.

As Amy walked away from Max, she let out a small howl. The pain was unmeasurable within her. She never thought she would love a man, and she did not love Max in the way that she was meant to. But she did love him, she loved him so much, even more so now that he had happily put his life on the line to ensure Amy's safety. He truly was her soul mate, even if Amy's life did not always match the way Baskerville thought it should Amy was happy that she had been paired with him. She would not have wanted to have been paired with anyone else.

Chapter 34

The path to the oak tree was a long and steep one.

Amy could see it in the distance, but she had been able to see it for miles now. It seemed that no matter how far Amy walked she never got any closer to it. She was on her own now. Unable to look for help to give her direction. She was on her own.

There were moments when Amy contemplated simply turning around and going back to Baskerville. At least, she had her family back there. Out here she had nothing. She had no one to look after her and no one to speak to. She truly was all alone. Amy understood that she would find new friends when she got to the safe place. She would be able to meet up with the Americans and see their way of life. But she would now always be alone. She would never be able to come back here, and she would never see the people she loved again.

This had always been the plan. To run away and not turn back, but when Amy had thought of this plan, she had people by her side. Never did she think she would be running away alone.

Just as she was almost giving up hope she came to a little stream. Amy was thirsty, she had only noticed now but she was very thirsty. She stopped by the stream to get a drink and decided to make camp here for the night. It was secluded enough that she would not be seen but at the same time open enough so that Amy could see if there was anyone headed her way.

She collected leaves and twigs to make a fire and filled up her bottle with water from the stream. She knew that she should boil the water before she drank it, but she did not really care. She had come to the decision now that if she died on the way then that was that. She would simply be found by a traveller and would never be named. Amy had made peace with that and was happy if that was the way it ended. She was purely following this tree for Max. As far as her plan went, she had given up.

She took her coat off and wrapped herself in it. This would have to suffice as a bed for the night. She fell asleep quickly, but her mind was filled with visions of those she had lost all through the night so that when she woke, she felt worse than she did when she had gone to sleep.

The fire had gone out when Amy awoke. It was cold, out in the open without any shelter. She had another drink from the stream and packed up her stuff. She was going to make it to the tree today, so she had to make sure she was full of strength.

While she had been asleep, she had come to a decision. She had lost too much to not pursue this now. She had lost too many people and too many things to not carry this on. There was nothing else she could do but carry on. Her home was no longer her home and the people who she cared about the most had gone. There was nothing left for her anywhere. She was going to have to start again. Start completely fresh. With new people and new things.

As she walked, she found herself humming. Humming the song that had been on the radio at the time of all this. The idea of this made her smile. The idea that her mind had taken her all the way back there. It was like her subconscious was telling her something. Something she couldn't quite decipher just yet. But something that was important and something that she knew she would have to take notice of it eventually.

Amy kept her focus on the oak tree in the distance the whole time she was walking. That was the only thing that was keeping her going. She had to get to that oak tree. She knew that the instructions to the rest of her life were within that tree. That tree was her only hope at a normal life. It was all she had left to some sort of reality within this world.

After what seemed like an eternity, the sun started to sink. Amy couldn't believe she had been walking for a full day. A full day without seeing anyone or anything. Not even a fly had buzzed past her. It was like the whole world was aware that they should not be near the boundary of Baskerville. Amy did not think that it went this far out, but obviously the American people were more scared of Baskerville than what was ever made out in the stories that were told within school.

She should have known really. Amy had only ever heard the tales from Baskerville. She had never even thought about the rest of the world and their reaction till now. She was looking at the barren landscape that had been left by the border and it all seemed to make sense. No one had come to rescue her because they were scared of what Baskerville would do if Americans tried to get into their grounds.

Just as Amy was about to give up hope and set up camp for another night, she saw it. The tree! She could not believe it. A whole day of aimless walking and she was finally at her destination. She had made it! She just had to make the next 100 yards and she would be there. Then she would hold the key to her freedom. She would hold the answer for years of pain.

As she approached the tree, she couldn't remember what Max had said. She was sure that he had told her where to look within the tree, but she could not remember. She looked and looked around the tree, but it was hopeless. There was nothing there. Nothing that would give the answer anyway. Nothing that would give Amy any hope. Nothing that would help her to escape the hell that was inside her head.

It did not take long, but eventually Amy gave up hope. That was it. Her last hope had become futile. She unpacked her small bag and once again wrapped herself in her coat and settled down for the night. She would not be finding her happily ever after. Amy told herself she would look again in the morning when the light of day would make it easier, but deep inside Amy knew that she was fighting a losing battle. It was all over. That was it. The dreams and the work had all been for nothing.

Morning came quicker this time. There had been no dreams. Nothing to speak of. Amy was sure that this meant that she had completely given up hope and that there was now nothing left for her in this world. This was the end and Amy could feel it.

She was unsure what to do now. Her only goal had been to get to the tree, but now she was here she did not know what her next move would be. She was stuck here. Stuck at this tree that had promised so much but did not deliver.

She began to pack up her bag and put back on her coat. As she picked up her coat, she heard a thud. Amy sprang into action. She removed her coat from the ground and began to dig. She dug till her hands were sore. It wasn't long until her fingers hit something hard.

As Amy dug further round the box in the ground her heart quickened. Could this be the hope that she had been wishing for. Could this be the thing that she had been wanting all this time. Was her happy ever after within this box?

After some manic digging, she managed to get the box out of the ground. It was not a very big box; the size of a shoebox would be a good description. But, unlike a shoebox, it was aged. Aged well, however, but aged. The wooden sides were warped and discoloured. It was clear that this box had been through a lot before it had been buried within the ground. This box had travelled and, like Amy, had clearly suffered through it.

Amy prised the box open and within it was a simple piece of paper.

Amy's heart jolted when she opened up the neatly folded paper.

If you're reading this, then the plan worked! I know this is a little cryptic, but I couldn't risk the monitors finding this piece of paper and understanding it. I also thought it would be good to have a treasure hunt type thing before you actually came to the house. I thought it would be fun!

Once you have read this you need to destroy it. I don't care how you do it, but destroy it as it will lead people straight to you if they find it, so it is crucial that they do not.

Keep walking, just keep walking. When you come to your favourite house, walk in.

Amy finished reading the piece of paper. She suddenly realised that she was shaking. Her stomach was churning. She turned away from the box and back to the hole, before being sick straight into the hole. The shock had smacked her in the face. There was nothing that could have prepared her for that.

That handwriting. That fucking handwriting.

Amy was not sure what it meant. She didn't know if this meant that Emma was alive or whether it had been written before the incident with the monitors. She was not clear on anything anymore. She could only do one thing. The one thing that she had been instructed to do. She carried on walking. She would walk and walk until she found her favourite house and then she would walk in. That would be the only way to put the rumours in her head to sleep. She would have to find out for herself.

Could Emma somehow be, okay? Or was Amy just being too optimistic. She had lost too much for any of this to be real.

Chapter 35

The walk was one of the longest walks of Amy's life. She just kept walking. She just kept going forward. She could not risk stopping. She knew if she stopped, she would never get going again. She knew that this was the last journey. No matter what. This would be last journey that she would be doing. Amy had promised herself. This was it. Life's last chance to show her that there was something for her in this world.

As Amy walked, she became aware of a small village that was coming into view. She could only assume that this was where the house would be. She walked towards the village sheepishly. She almost did not want to go into the village and find her favourite house. She did not want to walk into that house and find it empty. She was enjoying it within this world where she was nearly sure she knew the answers about Emma but there was a flicker of hope.

Amy did not want to lose that flicker. That small, small flicker of hope. That was all she had, and she was reluctant to let it go. To walk into that house would mean confirmation. Confirmation of all her doubts and fears. Amy was not ready. She had already gone through it once; she was unsure if she could go through it again.

The village was one of the prettiest places that Amy had ever been too. The houses were huddled around the cobbled streets as though it provided some sort of sustenance for them, in the middle of the street stood a wishing well that did not seem to be operational but was still a nice touch. The houses were all uniformly ununiform which was a charming touch to the place. Amy could feel that this was the place. This was where she was meant to be. This was where the house was. The safe house that Max had told her about, it was in here.

All the houses were very similar, except for one. This one was on the smaller side, and it was on the end of the row. It was slightly lower than the others suggesting it had lower ceilings. It was also slightly more ramshackled than the others. It looked like it had not been properly taken care of in a long time. It looked like it had simply been left to decay with the world. There were some touches within it though that told you that someone did love this house. The flower beds were filled with fresh flowers and the water tank was clearly full to the brim, suggesting that whoever lived there had just filled it up.

It was this one.

Amy did not even need a minute to think about it. This was the house. This was the house where everything would either be fixed or come crashing down around her. Amy did not know what to do. She didn't know whether to go into the house or run away. She was almost happier not knowing. She didn't want to know. She didn't want to know what had come of her life that she could have had. She did not want to know what she could have won, when she would have no one to share it with.

Amy approached the door but was hesitant to open it. She knew whatever happened, behind this door was the answer and good or bad, the answer was here. As she went to grab the cold steel handle, Amy was suddenly made aware of her breathing and heartrate. Both had increased to immeasurable heights as though she had just run a marathon. She hesitated a moment before opening the door. She needed to compose herself. She needed to be prepared for what lay behind this door.

Amy slowly turned the handle and opened the door. She pushed it slowly and it creaked in pain. As though it was rarely opened and objected greatly to the action asked of it.

Behind the door, was a very traditional cottage. The kind that Amy had always dreamed of living in. Baskerville was always a little too futuristic, whereas this cottage was at least 50 years behind. Amy was not even sure if there was hot water within this house. There was no sign of it. The floor was made of concrete slabs that were laid in a hexagon pattern. It was a nice touch to the very square room.

The kitchen was a simple one, with a large table in the middle of it. As Amy closed the door behind her, she realised how dark it was within these houses. She looked for the light switch and suddenly realised there wasn't one. How far ahead was Baskerville? Why had they kept all of this a secret from the rest of the world?

As Amy was becoming entranced with the little house, she heard footsteps.

Terror entered her body like a virus. She was not sure who that could be. What if she had got the wrong house? There was no way to confirm that she was in the right house until she met this person. She had been told to go into her favourite house and it was this one, there was no doubt, but what if that was not the one the person who wrote the note thought she would go into. What if she had got it wrong?

The footsteps came closer. This was it. This was the moment that Amy would discover if all of this had been worth it, or whether she would live out the rest of her days alone.

"I can't believe you have managed to get here. When we first came up with this plan, I did not think that it was going to be possible and then when the monitors found us and all that happened, I was sure that you were dead. How did you get away? How did you manage it? Do the monitors know where you are? Have you been followed? Where is Max? Oh, it is so good to see you!"

Emma was a whirlwind that Amy was just not ready for. She had fired all the questions at her. All the questions that Amy did not really know the answer to. The past few days had all been a blur, she could remember anything clearly anymore. She did not even know if it had been real!

The emotion was all too much. She could not carry on. She could not process all of this right not.

It was then that she fell. She finally fell.

It had all just become too much. She could not carry on anymore. Her body had given up.

Amy heard Emma's voice calling her name, but it was too late. She was already gone.

It was then that everything went black.

Chapter 36

When Amy awoke, she was not sure if the events within her memory had happened or if she had dreamt it. She was not even sure if her memory was reliable at this stage. She was a wreck. Her whole body ached.

There was a knock from the door. Amy panicked. What if she had remembered wrong? What if Emma wasn't here and she had been captured again by the monitors?

She could feel her heart rate quickening. What if her memory was wrong? What if the monitors did have her?

"Amy? Amy? Are you awake?"

Amy was coming out of her sleep, but she was not fully awake yet. She did not know how to react to the voice that coming to her. She knew that voice and she knew that voice meant safety, but she was not sure who it was.

"Amy please. Let me know that you can hear me?"

The desperation in her voice was growing. She was almost shouting now. Emma was sitting at the side of the bed, shaking Amy. She needed her to wake up. She needed answers that only Amy could give her. She needed her to give her the story that she was missing. She needed to fully understand what had happened and why it had happened.

Amy began to wake up. Her brain became less fuzzy, and she was starting to understand what was happening around her. She was beginning to understand exactly who was talking to her and what they were saying. For the first time in a long time, Amy began to believe that Emma might be alive. Emma might be alive, and she might be here with her now, in the safe house. She could be here, and if she was, she was on the side of her bed right now.

As Amy opened her eyes she was almost hoping, praying, that she was right. If she opened her eyes and found anyone other than Emma, then she did not know what she would do. After what had happened over the past few days, she needed a boost. She needed to know that it had all been worth it, it had been worth the heart break and the loss and there was a reason that she had done all the fighting.

She did it, she finally built up the courage to open her eyes. When she did, she was filled with elation. She felt as though the world was now a nicer place. Her lungs filled with air and felt as though they would lift her whole body off the ground. Amy had never felt like this before. She had never had the elation that she was feeling right now.

She had never had a reason to be as happy as she was right now, but she was there and feeling it. The love of her life was standing in front of her, trying to wake her up. She could not believe it, Emma was alive! The last time she had seen her she was being carried away under a sheet as though she was dead. She was dead, Amy had seen her. She was sure that she was dead.

Amy had so many questions. How did this happen? How had Emma survived the monitors attack when it was so clear that she was dead?

"I can't believe you're here! Finally! It has been so long; I can't tell you how much I have missed you; it is unreal! I just can't believe it. Tell me, you need to tell me. Tell me everything! What have I missed, what has happened, how did you get away? Sorry, I know, that was too many questions. I will go and make some tea and we can catch up over that!"

Emma had thrown everything at Amy, so much so that Amy did not know what to do. She had just awoken to the sight of Emma, who she was sure was dead and then fired with questions. She was frozen. Frozen to the bed. She just didn't know what to do!

She did not know how to react to everything around her. She didn't know what to do with all the information that had been thrown at her.

Amy had a few moments to compose herself before Emma came back with the tea. She would get herself out of bed and ready to talk. She would have to give Emma something in order for her to gain the information that she needed from Emma.

Emma had walked down the stairs and put the kettle on the hob. She was unsure how she was going to begin this conversation. She understood that she was going to have to have a conversation with Amy about what had happened when she left the monitors, but she was unsure how she was going to bring it up. How would she explain why she was the one that was saved while Amy was left in prison to be hanged?

She had to tell her somehow as Amy would wonder how she got out of prison and none of that would make sense without admitting that she got help. She got the help that was meant to come and get Amy.

The kettle whistled suddenly, like an alarm. Telling Emma that her time to get her story straight was over. She had run out of time. She would have to now come to terms with what she had done and admit it to the woman she loved more than anything in the world!

She grabbed the tea bags and made the tea, the cups clinked together as she walked, like a countdown till she would have to face her fears.

Emma slowly pushed the door open until she saw Amy sitting on the bed. She had managed to get up. Emma was glad, she was worried as to how tired she would be after going through what she had been through.

Emma did not know what to say. How was she going to ask all the questions that she needed the answers to? There was no way for her to ask all these questions without overwhelming Amy. She might just simply have to start from the beginning and explain everything about how she survived the monitors and how she got out of Baskerville in the first place. That was what Amy would want to know. That was the first thing she would have to talk about when they had this conversation.

Amy was sitting there, propped up by the pillows. It was clear that had the pillows not been there she would have collapsed. She was completely reliant on them. She had none of her own strength. Nothing that would support her upright. Her body had given up on trying to keep everything going.

She had never looked so pale either. That was what Emma kept noticing. She had never looked so pale in the whole time that she had known her. This worried Emma as she was not sure what she would do if Amy was ill. It did not look like Max had made it and she did not know anyone this side of the fence so how could she trust someone at this early stage?

Emma knew that she could not allow her imagination to get the better of her and that she could only work with what she had. It might not be an issue, Amy might just be tired, and if that was the case Emma would be able to handle that.

Amy muttered something under her breathe. Emma struggled to hear her; she was inaudible. It was almost like she was trying to say something important, but Emma could not hear her.

Amy was unsure why Emma was not responding to her. It was almost like she was ignoring her. She knew that she wouldn't be, but that was what it felt like. Amy tried to speak again, but this time she was audible and this time she shouted at the top of her lungs. There was no way that you could not hear her.

"Max is dead!" Amy erupted.

Chapter 37

Now that the words had left her mouth, it was like it all suddenly became real. The tears that she had been holding back all this time erupted out of her like a volcano, pouring like lava down her face. How she had held on for this long Amy was unsure, but she could not hold on now, it had gone. It was too late. She had let it out now.

The emotion came over her like a wave. There was nothing she could do about it. The emotion had been set free. It was taking over her like a wave of misery. A wave of misery that had been kept at bay by purely ignoring it.

Emma did not know how to react. How did she respond to this new information? How would she tell her that it was all okay? It was never going to be okay. Max had put his life on the line to make this happen, but he had died. He had wasted his life for them to be free.

Emma knew that she had to just be there for Amy and explain that everything happens for a reason. But mostly she had to tell Amy that it was not her fault that Max was dead, it was not her fault that any of this had happened. It was never her idea in the first place. She did not come up with the plan, she had just gone a long with it.

"Amy, you cannot blame yourself for what happened. It was never your fault. None of this is your fault."

She needed her to understand that she was not to blame. She needed to know that everything that had happened was not her fault. Amy needed to know that none of this was because of her. She needed to know that even though bad things had happened, it was not because of her. Nothing Amy could have done would have stopped this from happening.

Amy was listening to Emma as she tried to comfort her. She was listening intently as she explained everything to her. But she knew, deep down, that Emma was simply saying these things to make her feel better. There was no way that would work unfortunately. Even Amy knew that it would not work. It would take some words to stop the pain that she was feeling, even if those words came from Emma, she would not be able to supress these feelings for much longer.

Amy could not control her emotion at this point. She knew that she had to let it out. She knew that she had to understand that Max was not coming. She needed to know that this was it. The end of the road. There was nothing that she would be able to do in order to change the events that had happened over the last few days. But there was one thing that was keeping her at peace. One thing that seemed to make all the suffering worth it in the end. She was with Emma.

She was with Emma alone!

This was something that she had never had before. They had always been looking over their shoulders and making sure that they had not been seen together. They were always living in fear. But that didn't have to happen anymore. It didn't need to happen because they were finally out of Baskerville. They were finally out of the controlling state that had ruled their lives. They were free to do what they wanted.

If nothing else, that was a cause for celebration.

"Emma, I know that it has taken us a lot to get here, and I know that we are currently in a weird situation because a lot of people have been hurt for us to be here. But do you remember what Max said before we started all this? He said that we had to be grateful for everything, even it came because of something wrong we did. Even if what we did was wrong, which on paper it is, what we have got out of it is magical and there is nothing more in the world that I want other than to spend eternity with you. I could not imagine anything more that I would rather do."

"So, I know how sad it is and I know that it is not my fault, but I also know that Max would want us to carry on and not mope around. He would want us to be together and happy. He would not want us to be sitting like this being sad over him. We must be happy. I know it is hard right now, but we have to make the most out of this opportunity that we have been given, otherwise, what is the point? We could still be in Baskerville if we are not going to act. So, let's do it! Let's live together and enjoy our new life that has been gifted to us!"

Emma knew that Amy was right. She just could not believe the change in her. She could not believe that she had gone from screaming about Max to deciding this, in a flash. It was like she knew that Max wanted them to be happy and she was determined to make that happen. Emma was glad to see the change.

Knowing that Amy had finally accepted that she was not to blame for Max's death and that she could finally be happy within her new life.

Chapter 38

A few months had passed, and the girls were settling into their new life. They both had managed to find jobs and were working to buy a house a little closer the city. Now that there were not so many rules, they had decided that they could stand living a little closer to other people. It was a weird sensation at first, not having to hide from people. But they soon got used to it and were now enjoying their life and looking forward. It was like a weight had been lifted off their shoulders and they were finally free to live their life the way they wanted to. There was nothing that Amy wanted more than for Emma to be happy with her new life.

Both girls had used their skills differently within the new world. Emma was working at a bakery creating all kinds of fancy cakes for the people of the town. She would make them for birthdays and weddings or for whatever occasion needed a cake. She was happy within her job for the first time ever. She did not have to worry about the others that were around her and she certainly did not have to control them to gain her money. It was a nice relaxing break for her from the stress of being a monitor, as she had been within Baskerville.

Amy took a different approach. She wanted to carry on using her skills that she had learnt in monitor school, but she did not want to still be part of controlling society. Luckily, she realised that within America this was not the case. The police were there to protect not to control to this allowed Amy to become a part of the solution rather than the problem. Amy was very happy within the police, and she was working on getting to the top of the ladder and becoming a detective chief inspector one day. She had a long way to go, but at least she was doing something meaningful with her life.

Both girls had started over within their new life and both girls were happy. They could not believe that it had all worked. They had managed to escape from the cruelty of Baskerville. Amy sometimes thought about those who she had left behind. She thought about her parents, not knowing why she had left and not knowing what to do now their little girl was gone.

She would have been as good as dead in the eyes of Baskerville. It had probably been announced as such to the community. Amy could only hope that her parents knew different and that they knew that she had to do it. She had to run away. She could not stay within that place and get arrested simply because of who she loved. The notion was ridiculous when you say it like that!

It was getting into winter now. The sun was starting to disappear earlier and the green leaves on the trees were starting to disappear. Amy was coming home from a particularly rough day at work. She was so ready to come home and plonk onto the sofa.

As she walked down the garden path towards the door, the smell of fresh bread was dancing into her nose. Emma must have got home early and started making some bread for tea. She was good like that; she did use her talents well within the kitchen. She was a natural baker and with everything that she had learnt from working at the bakery, she was becoming even better.

Amy opened the front door, only to be hit by the warm waft of scent. The fresh bread sounded very nearly ready, and Amy suddenly realised how hungry she was.

"The bread smells amazing babe, is it a new one?"

Amy was always the first to compliment Emma on her cooking. Even after a hard day at work, it was the best thing to come home to something being cooked in the oven.

"Yes new one today, I hope you like it. I have put apple slices within it to add some sweetness, and to try and get at least some fruit into you!"

Emma had always been healthier than Amy, but now that they were no longer on rations Amy had almost gone crazy. She was loving the food that was available within America and was simply lapping it up!

Emma got the bread out of the oven and began to slice it up. The scent filled the house. It was strong but there was just a hint of apple within there, although Amy was not sure if she would have noticed it had Emma not pointed it.

As Emma was getting the plates out, Amy turned on the television.

The tele spurted into action, Amy watched the news every evening while eating tea, it drove Emma mad.

"Babe, can we watch something a little cheerier tonight. All that bad news is killing me"

Something cut her off. She stood there focused on the television set as a woman was stood giving her report.

Behind her people were running for their lives while aeroplanes were shooting at them from above. It was absolute chaos; nothing could have prepared them for this. The streets were unrecognisable with everyone running in them. There was too much movement for Emma to make anything out within the picture. But she knew this place. This place was far too familiar.

All this terror was happening within Baskerville.

Chapter 39

"We just have to think about it logically."

Amy was trying to be reasonable with Emma as she began to pace round the house.

"There is nothing we can do that is going to change this, I promise you."

Amy knew that this was not the case. All they wanted was them, but she was not about to self-surrender when she had gotten so used to being free and enjoying her life. This was bigger than her. It was bigger than she could ever be.

The woman on the tv was giving everyone a brief overview of everything and what had been happening. It had become clear that Baskerville had been threatening America for far too long and something had to stop.

America had decided to do something.

America had declared war.

"They can't have declared war on Baskerville. Do they not know about the nuclear?"

Amy knew what Emma was saying. She was repeating what had been told to us for generations. The fact that no one would ever be able to touch Baskerville because if they ever did, they would be able to destroy the whole world with one bomb. But Amy was curious about this. If they had this strong weapon then surely, they would have just detonated it at the end of the first great war, then none of this would have had to happen.

"I am not so sure if the nuclear is real. I have been thinking about this for a while. If the nuclear was real, then there would be no problem and Baskerville would have detonated it years ago, but they haven't so it makes me think there never was any and it has all just been a ploy to stop the war and make them look like the peaceful ones when really, they needed time to prepare before they resumed again, and now they're resuming!"

It was not the most bonkers of ideas and Emma had certainly heard more crazy ones, but it was something to think about. If Baskerville did not have

174

nuclear in the first place, then there would be nothing to fear. Nothing to worry about and nothing they could do.

Yes, the monitors were tough, but so were the American Army. Amy couldn't see this lasting very long.

And just as the girls relaxed and began to feel safe again. Just as the whole world was thinking that Baskerville was all talk about nuclear. And that the world would be able to go on as normal. Just as the dust had settled and people started to forget about Baskerville and their threat.

That was when the bang came. A bang that was so great it shook the whole world, a bang so great that it was heard on the moon.

A bang that detonated the world.